Praise for A

"Hold on to your pith helmets. The next popular young adult book series could be *The Journals of Thaddeaus Shockpocket*."

Unsie Zuege, *The Chanhassen Villager*

"*The Journals of Thadeaus Schockpocket* is a rip-roaring adventure for young readers... Thaddeaus Shockpocket offers readers an alternate world; a world of ancient monsters, airships, underrated yet lovable inventors and highly intelligent, fearless females. In short, there is everything for the intelligent, adventure-loving youth to enjoy!"

Leslie Orton, *The Aether Review of Books*

From Amazon.com

"...open a new tin of biscuits (Tweak's favorite), brew yourself a cup of Ceylon tea and settle down for one rollicking adventure after another from The Journals of Thaddeaus Shockpocket. Enjoy. I did, and I'm not even a kid. It's tickety-boo."

"The 'inventions' and 'gadgets' depicted in the book are simply brilliant. I enjoyed the characters, the humor, and the hilarious situations in which the shockpocket family find themselves."

"This book makes you feel that ANYTHING is possible if you are creative and put your mind to it!"

"Entertaining, full of puns, word play and an off-beat sense of humor. A great read, and am looking forward to more Shockpocket (mis)adventures."

To KASEN,

IN THE SPIRIT of
SCIENCE & ADVENTURE

HENRY L. WALTON

The Journals of
Thaddeaus Shockpocket
Victoria

Henry L. Walton

Illustrated by
William Kevin Petty

**CALUMET
EDITIONS**

Chanhassen, Minnesota, USA

CALUMET EDITIONS

FIRST EDITION MARCH 2015

The Journals of

Thaddeaus Shockpocket —
VICTORIA

Book design by Gary Lindberg
Cover design by William Kevin Petty

Visit the author at: Shockpocket.com

Follow the author at: @henrywalton77

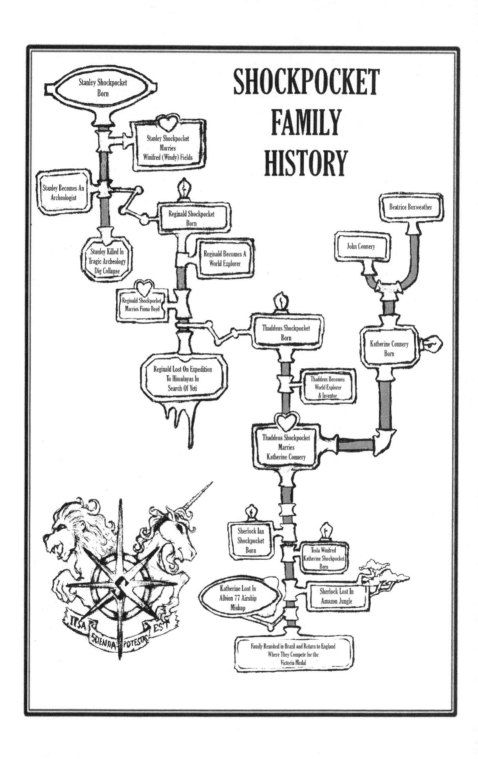

SHOCKPOCKET
FAMILY
HISTORY

Stanley Shockpocket Born

Stanley Shockpocket Marries Winifred (Windy) Fields

Stanley Becomes An Archeologist

Stanley Killed In Tragic Archeology Dig Collapse

Reginald Shockpocket Born

Reginald Becomes A World Explorer

Reginald Shockpocket Marries Fiona Boyd

Reginald Lost On Expedition To Himalayas In Search Of Yeti

Thaddeus Shockpocket Born

Thaddeus Becomes World Explorer & Inventor

Beatrice Boxweather

John Connery

Katherine Connery Born

Thaddeus Shockpocket Marries Katherine Connery

Sherlock Ian Shockpocket Born

Tesla Winifred Katherine Shockpocket Born

Katherine Lost In Albion 77 Airship Mishap

Sherlock Lost In Amazon Jungle

Family Reunited in Brazil and Return to England Where They Compete for the Victoria Medal

IPSA SCIENTIA POTESTAS EST

Dear reader

I PRESUME THAT YOU HAVE READ "THE JOURNALS OF THADDEAUS SHOCKPOCKET - ALBION 77" AND YOUR CURIOSITY AS TO THE FATE OF THE SHOCKPOCKET FAMILY AFTER RETURNING FROM THE DARKEST REGION OF THE AMAZON JUNGLE HAS NOT ONLY KEPT YOU IN SUSPENSE BUT DRIVEN YOU UNCONTROLLABLY TO FIND THE BOOK YOU NOW HOLD IN YOUR HANDS.

OR, FAR LESS LIKELY, YOU HAVE NEVER HEARD OF THADDEAUS SHOCKPOCKET, HAVE NO IDEA WHAT I AM BLATHERING ABOUT, AND ARE NOW QUESTIONING WHAT ON EARTH PROVOKED YOU TO PULL THIS TOME FROM THE SHELF AND READ THE INTRODUCTION.

IN THAT CASE, LET ME GIVE YOU A LITTLE BACKGROUND. I AM PROFESSOR THADDEAUS SHOCKPOCKET AND AM AN EXPLORER AND INVENTOR ALONG WITH MY WIFE KATHERINE, SON SHERLOCK, AND DAUGHTER TWEAK. TWEAK AND I DECIDED TO PUBLISH MY SCIENTIFIC JOURNALS LAST YEAR AFTER A SERIES OF ADVERSE EVENTS LED US TO BELIEVE THE SHOCKPOCKET FAMILY LINE MAY SOON COME TO AN END. JUST FIVE YEARS PRIOR, MY THEN TEN-YEAR-OLD SON SHERLOCK DISAPPEARED INTO THE

AMAZON JUNGLE WHILE WE WERE ON AN EXPEDITION SCOUTING FOR HERBAL REMEDIES. AN UNFORTUNATE MISUNDERSTANDING OF LOCAL CUSTOMS RESULTED IN ME ACCIDENTALLY PRESENTING SHERLOCK TO A LOCAL TRIBAL CHIEF AS A GIFT AND WE HAD NOT BEEN ABLE TO LOCATE HIM SINCE. THEN, LAST SPRING, I LOST MY WIFE IN A TRAGIC ACCIDENT. OUR FAMILY AIRSHIP ALBION 77 BROKE ITS MOORING LINES AND KATHERINE FLEW AWAY, UNABLE TO RETURN TO THE GROUND BECAUSE I HAD FAILED TO INSTALL AN ELEVATION CONTROL HANDLE ON THE SHIP. AFTER SHE DRIFTED AWAY FROM THE ENGLISH ISLES, WE ONLY HEARD FROM HER ONCE AS SHE PASSED OVER EGYPT AND TRANSMITTED A MESSAGE ON THE BALLOON'S SHOCKPOCKET TYPOTELEGRAPH.

WITH THE DISAPPEARANCE OF THE ONLY TWO OTHER MEMBERS OF THE SHOCKPOCKET FAMILY, MY TWELVE YEAR OLD DAUGHTER TWEAK AND I DECIDED TO PUBLISH THE JOURNALS AND NOTES IN ORDER TO DOCUMENT OUR DISCOVERIES AND KEEP THE SHOCKPOCKET NAME ALIVE IN EVENT WE ALSO SUCCUMBED TO DISASTROUS MISFORTUNE. FOR SEVERAL MONTHS TWEAK AND I LIVED ALONE WITH OUR GOLDEN RETRIEVER SHANDY AND TALKING CHIMPANZEE NANA WHILE WE CONTINUED OUR SEARCH FOR SHERLOCK AND KATHERINE AND CREATED SEVERAL NEW INVENTIONS ALONG THE WAY.

AS LUCK WOULD HAVE IT, WE FOUND SHERLOCK IN THE AMAZON JUNGLE SAFE AND SOUND WITH THE VERY NATIVE TRIBE THAT HAD ADOPTED HIM THOSE MANY YEARS BACK. HEARING OF HIS MOTHER'S DISAPPEARANCE, SHERLOCK DECIDED TO STAY WITH HIS NEW FAMILY AND TWEAK AND I RETURNED TO ENG-

LAND ALONE. BUT THEN, IN AN EVEN GREATER TURN OF LUCK AND GOOD FORTUNE, KATHERINE AND THE RUN-AWAY AIRSHIP ALBION 77 CAME DOWN SAFELY IN THE VERY SAME JUNGLE LOCATION AS SHERLOCK'S VILLAGE AFTER CIRCLING MOST OF THE WORLD OUT OF CONTROL. KATHERINE SENT WORD FROM BRAZIL AND OUR FAMILY REUNITED.

IN THESE PAGES, I HAVE COLLECTED FURTHER STORIES OF KATHERINE, SHERLOCK, TWEAK, AND YOURS TRULY AFTER OUR RETURN TO LOVELY ENGLAND AND THE SHOCKPOCKET ESTATE WHERE WE CONTINUE TO EXPERIMENT, EXPLORE, AND INVENT NEW THINGS TO BETTER THE WORLD.

YOURS IN THE SPIRIT OF SCIENCE AND ADVENTURE,

PROFESSOR THADDEAUS SHOCKPOCKET
WORLD EXPLORER AND INVENTOR

The Victoria Medal

Sunday, November 28

What a brilliant day it has been. This morning, when Sherlock, Tweak and I gathered at the table for breakfast, Katherine surprised us with a fantastic treat of Belgium style waffles accompanied by a large plate of sizzling bacon. Tweak has loved waffles since she first tasted them in Brussels as a little girl. She covers the waffles with heaps of strawberry preserves and then tops them with large spoonsful of whipped cream.

Today, Katherine rose from bed early and quietly made her way down to the kitchen to prepare a surprise breakfast while the rest of us were still sleeping. I was especially delighted with the unexpected delicacy until it dawned on me that today must be a special day and I had totally forgotten what special day it was. Not one to be flustered by such an event, I immediately did the only thing that one is obliged to in a situation such as this. I immediately ran to the greenhouse, located my finest rose bush, cut twelve long stem roses, then went to the garden shed, placed the fresh cut roses in the fanciest vase I could find and brought the floral arrangement back into the dining room accompanied by a card that read "To my dearest Kate, Happy November 28th. Who could ever forget this special day?"

The children also could not think of any special event that had occurred on November 28th. They agreed that this was the best defensive plan of action.

When Kate re-entered the dining room with a fresh pot of tea she saw the flowers on the table and her face absolutely lit up. "Why Thaddeaus, what a nice thought to place fresh roses on the table." Then she saw the card and read it. Upon reading the handwritten note, her face took on an expression of slight confusion. She looked up and said, "Oh my, is today special?" She paused a moment to think and then said, "I must admit that I am terribly embarrassed to say I do not recall November 28th being a special day. You know that I am usually quite good at remembering special occasions but I must ask, what are we celebrating?"

The children and I glanced at each other. Now we were all confused. I spoke up. "But we thought, with the special breakfast and your bright spirit this morning, it must be a special day. We just could not think of what it was and didn't want you to think we forgot."

Kate laughed, "No you sillies, it is not special for anything that has occurred in the past. However, I have a feeling it just may be a special day in the future."

Kate went over to a side table and picked up a newspaper I had not read.

"Look at the article on page three. I think it could be an opportunity for our next expedition."

I opened the paper to page three and immediately spotted the reason for Kate's excitement.

English Royal Society of Scientific Research and Global Exploration Announces Award

This week, the English Royal Society of Scientific Research and Global Exploration announced a new award to honor breakthroughs in all disciplines of science. The award is called the Victoria Medal for Scientific Discovery. Dr. Erlenmeyer Beakersniff, society chairman and spokesman, noted that the organization has historically presented individual annual awards for achievements in the key disciplines of chemistry, biology, physics, and archeology. The new award will be open to all branches of science and will recognize the single greatest discovery of the year among all of the disciplines. In addition to a medal, the award will include a significant cash prize.

The scientific community has reacted with strong praise for the award saying it will finally recognize those areas of exploration that have typically been dismissed as unimportant or frivolous. Only the famed archeologist Wallace Bogglesworth has criticized the award saying, "This new award is offensive to the practitioners of true science.

Opening the competition up to all areas of exploration and discovery will bring every nutter and loony out of the woodwork. Those who spend their days dreaming about space travel and other such nonsense only waste valuable time and energy that could be better spent in traditional studies. These people are an embarrassment to proper scientists such as me."

In spite of his dismissal of the award, Dr. Bogglesworth predicted that, while many will try to win the Victoria Medal, it is he who will be victorious with another discovery in the field of Egyptology.

Katherine was right to celebrate the news. The award was absolutely brilliant and a perfect reason to begin our next quest. Even if we did not know what that would be.

After reading the newspaper article to myself, I read it out loud to Tweak and Sherlock and they agreed that we should, indeed, try to make the greatest discovery of the year and win the Victoria Medal for Scientific Discovery. Winning the award would mean that the Shockpocket family would be recognized as real scientists, and the cash prize would help pay for new laboratory equipment to invent more devices to improve the world.

This afternoon, we gathered in the study to create a list of possibilities for a discovery that could win the award. Our study is a multipurpose room that not only houses the Shockpocket library, but also serves as a gathering place for meetings. It is also where we relax at the end of the day to talk, read, and play games. The oak paneled room is somewhat narrow, but makes up for the lack of width by being quite long and tall, rising up two stories to a glass-paned ceiling that provides a wondrous view of the day or nighttime sky. Large windows run the length of one side of the room to provide panoramic views of the grass airfield and the Shockpocket airplane and airship hangars on the far side. On the wall opposite the windows stands a great stone fireplace that climbs to the ceiling. The fireplace has an opening wide enough to consume entire logs up to four feet in length and is tall enough for Tweak to walk into without touching her head. To each side of the fireplace, shelves filled with thousands of books rise from the floor to a height far beyond anyone's reach. A ladder, fitted with wheels at the base, is attached to a brass rail that runs across the top of the bookshelves the entire width of the room. For anyone with the fortitude to climb it, the tall ladder provides access to books on the highest shelves, though it tends to wobble and roll sideways a tich when one leans out to reach for a book.

At the far end of the room, one may peer down into the study from a railing located along a hallway on the second level of our manor. Directly below the rail, a blackboard runs the entire width of the room. In front of the chalk dust and note-covered surface sits a large oak table and several wood chairs. It is here, in front of the blackboard, that we gather to plan our experiments and expeditions.

Today, as Tweak, Sherlock, and Katherine settled into their chairs in front of the black wall, I picked up a piece of chalk and wrote in large letters:

IDEAS TO WIN THE VICTORIA MEDAL

As I set the chalk down, Tweak spoke up. "I suggest we make a discovery in the field of cryptozoology."

She made the statement as though it was the only logical idea. She even stood up to take a bow as she finished her proclamation.

"Why would we want to make a discovery in the field of mythical creatures?" Katherine asked.

I also wondered why Tweak would suggest crypto-zoology when we had made several discoveries in more traditional fields in the past and should be able to do so again.

She answered, looking somewhat annoyed. "Because we already know one mythical creature that really exists. We only need to go back to Loch Ness and this time collect solid evidence that a giant serpent lives there. The locals have claimed its existence for hundreds of years but no one has ever been able to show any proof. If we get photographs of the creature we would be the first, and that certainly would be a major discovery worthy of the Victoria Medal."

Tweak made a good point. Without further discussion, we all agreed that we should enter the competition in the field of cryptozoology. We will build a boat specially designed for the expedition and return to Loch Ness to search again for Nessie.

Saturday, December 11

The ceremony to announce the entrants for the Victoria Medal competition took place on the front steps of the English Royal Society of Scientific Research and Global Exploration. The E.R.S.S.R.G.E. building is located in the heart of London and is quite an imposing structure. A long climb of white marble steps leads up to a gathering area in front of a pair of tall oak entryway doors. Several great white stone columns frame the entrance as they rise up to an ornate marble overhang that protects the entire area from rain.

Today, a dark wood podium was positioned at the top of the steps in the center of the gathering area. On the front of the pedestal hung a green banner that bore the gold embroidered insignia of the English Royal Society of Scientific Research and Global Exploration and to each side stood six members of the judging committee. What an odd collection of men! Some were rather short and round while others were tall and skinny, the tall ones looking even loftier in their towering top hats.

Behind the podium stood the one and only Dr. Erlenmeyer Beakersniff. Even though he did not wear a hat, Dr. Beakersniff was easily the tallest and most lanky fellow in the group. With his narrow topcoat and head of long white hair that stuck out in all directions, he reminded me of a dandelion that had gone to seed. I told Katherine that I was tempted to blow at his head to see if his hair would scatter in the wind. She kicked me hard in the shin.

A small band played an assortment of rousing tunes until Dr. Beakersniff signaled for them to stop and then raised his hand to quiet the crowd. When the onlookers had quieted down, Dr. Beakersniff began reading the list of scientists that had entered their names to compete for the Victoria Medal. The list was long and represented many of the finest men and women from all families of science.

When Dr. Beakersniff announced that I would be attempting to make a discovery in the field of cryptozoology, I was deeply filled with feelings of honor and pride. That was until Wallace Bogglesworth yelled out, "Surely you jest. Thaddeaus Shockpocket should not even be allowed into this competition. His chosen field of cryptozoology is a farce."

The crowd became silent. Time seemed to stand still and all eyes turned to me.

Wallace continued, "You, Thaddeaus Shockpocket, are responsible for single-handedly ruining my first Egyptian dig several years ago. In addition to that, during your own expedition in the Amazon Basin several years later, you unintentionally presented your ten-year-old son as a gift to a tribal chief, and then lost contact with him for several years. And last year you overinflated your airship Albion 77 and launched your lovely wife Katherine off on an out-of-control solo balloon voyage half way around the world. It was I, Wallace Bogglesworth, who found your wife and son in the jungle and made it possible for your family to reunite. My man, you are not a scientist. You are a walking disaster."

Murmurs rippled through the gathering. Then Tweak yelled out for all to hear, "Yes, but he also invented organic pink hair coloring. And a method of relocating nuisance rabbits using miniature catapults." She paused a moment to think, "And, and the Buffler personal odor modification device."

She puffed out her chest in pride as waves of laughter rose into the air.

Wallace simply shook his head and said, "I think that makes my point."

Dr. Beakersniff looked annoyed as he addressed Wallace, "Dear sir, it is not our place to judge fellow scientists. If Thaddeaus Shockpocket is indeed as incompetent as you suggest, then he will have no chance of winning the prize. On the other hand, if he does make the greatest discovery of the year, then all of us, including you, will have to recognize that he is indeed a legitimate scientist. Am I clear?"

Wallace replied loudly, "Clear as a window." And then muttered under his breath, "A very cloudy window."

The announcement ceremony ended with Dr. Bea-kersniff wishing all of the Victoria Medal entrants the best of luck and then leading the crowd in a round of three cheers followed by more music from the band.

After the ceremony, we spent the afternoon wander-ing through the shops of London and admiring the hol-iday lights and decorations. At four o'clock we paused for a wonderful cream tea in Hyde Park where we watched the swans gliding about the pond. The water and gliding birds took my thoughts to our next expedi-tion on Loch Ness and I pictured the look on Wallace Bogglesworth's face should we win the Victoria Medal for proving the Loch Ness beast is real. I calculate that we will be able complete construction of our new explo-ration boat in about three months. We will make our expedition in the Spring.

Painting Sheep

Monday, March 14

I must confess that I have a bit of a problem when it comes to focusing on one thing at a time. This occurs regularly when others are speaking to me and their conversation goes on and on, far beyond the point of being interesting. It seems such a waste of time to concentrate only on what someone is telling me when I can clearly accomplish more by pondering additional topics at the same time. Normally this habit does not create a problem as I simply nod my head or say yes in agreement to whatever someone is saying when-ever they pause, believing that I am actually listening to them. However, not listening properly does cause the occasional sticky situation, typically involving a conversation with Kate. It is particularly embarrass-ing when I have just given my customary head nod to Kate and she excitedly responds, "Seriously? I never thought you would agree to that." That's when I realize that I have no idea what she has been going on about for the past several minutes or what I have just agreed to.

Not listening closely to Katherine played a key role in my search for the perfect paint for sheep.

The sheep paint project began when Kate told me of a newspaper article about the popularity of painting sheep. As she went on about the phenomenon I began daydreaming but had heard enough of the story to conclude that painting sheep was quite in style and people were paying a lot of money for painted sheep. It occurred to me that I could use the knowledge I had gained from developing Thaddeaus Shockpocket's All Organic Hair Coloring to formulate a paint specifically for sheep wool. It would not be a difficult task and, if the trend of painting sheep was as popular as it sounded, it would be worth a lot of money.

Truth be told, I was a bit puzzled at the whole 'painted sheep' craze and could only think of two reasons why anyone would paint their sheep. The most practical reason could be to tint the lamb's wool before shearing. That would eliminate the need to dye it later when it was made into cloth. The second and less practical reason could be that people have developed a fondness for the sight of multicolored sheep grazing in their fields. While less practical, I had to admit that a field of colored sheep could be quite pleasing to the eye. Either way, the reason for the trend was not important.

I had a new discovery to make and would set off forthwith to do so.

As I endeavored to develop the new sheep paint I found that wool reacts to Shockpocket's All Organic Hair Coloring solutions differently than human hair. Not only does the dye not color the lamb's wool in a similar fashion but the sheep seem to love the flavor of the colored wool and chew off their coats. I tasted it myself and cannot imagine what the sheep find so appealing. I found it to be quite foul and it reminds me of when I was a youngster and would chew on the sleeve of my wool coat whenever I was nervous. I clearly remember that awful taste! But the sheep seem to like it and that forced me to create a completely new formula that tasted differently.

I also needed to invent a device to apply the paint quickly since the test sheep tended to become disturbed whenever I was painting them. Chasing them around the lab as I brushed the paint onto their coats made for too much work and was simply not practical.

Lastly, the paint needed to dry quickly as the fuzzy animals would rub against my laboratory walls immediately after being painted and wipe most of the color off. This left large streaks of bright paint that ran across the walls at a height of two to three feet above the floor. After several attempts, I successfully developed a broad range of paints that not only dried quickly but could be easily applied with the use of a spray-pump gun. The result was splendid. The paint looked brilliant on the sheep and no more paint ended up on my laboratory walls.

I did not want word of my new product to accidentally get out before I was ready to formally launch it, so my family only knew that I was conducting research that involved watching paint dry.

Finally, when I had completed the new paint formula and was certain I had a successful product, I called everyone into the family study for a special announcement. When they were all properly seated, I declared that I was about to show them what may very well be my best creation to date. The three fidgeted in their seats as I excused myself to retrieve some samples of my latest invention. A few moments later I returned, followed by three of the best looking sheep I have ever seen. One was painted bright red, one a deep shade of royal blue, and one, just to make an extra special presentation, was painted with the British flag on his side.

To say the introduction made an impression would be an understatement. Tweak was excited to see the colored lambs. She danced as she exclaimed that they were absolutely brilliant. Sherlock looked puzzled and asked exactly what my new invention was—and, by the way, why did I paint three of our sheep? Katherine just stared at the sheep blankly, blinked rapidly, and said nothing.

I turned toward Katherine, "Kate. I would like to thank you for being the one who inspired me to develop our latest product to improve the world, Thaddeaus Shockpocket's Sheep Paint."

Her face remained mostly blank but now showed some puzzlement. "Really? I don't recollect ever saying that I wanted colored sheep."

I responded, "But you did, silly. Don't you recall when you told me about the newspaper article? The one telling of the latest trend of painting sheep? I thought about it and decided it was only logical to use the Shockpocket Organic Hair Colors as a basis for a whole new line of sheep paints."

It is difficult to describe the look my dearest Kate gave me as I completed my explanation. I guess you could call it amusement. Combined with a little disbelief. Topped off with a bit of profound sympathy. She placed her hand over her mouth to stifle a laugh and then said. "Oh, my dearest Thaddeaus. I think your invention is absolutely brilliant, but I hesitate to tell you something that may dampen your spirits a tich."

What could dampen my spirits? Over two years of watching paint dry was more than worth it to create paints for all those people painting sheep.

She continued, "Thaddeaus, I did indeed tell you that the latest trend is painting sheep. And it continues to be a very popular. However, I think you missed one minor detail."

What could I have missed?

"Do you recall, in all of our recent travels, ever seeing any sheep in any field in any color other than natural white or perhaps brown or black.

Come to think of it, I had not.

"And as you spent time developing your fabulous sheep paint, didn't you ever wonder, if sheep painting is so popular, why you have never seen a painted sheep?"

Again, I had not.

"I am afraid you may not have been listening very well when I told you about the popularity of painted sheep. The latest craze can be seen in all of the modern art shops. Artists are adding sheep to their paintings of landscapes. Now, everyone wants to own a watercolor or oil painting of sheep grazing in fields. In fact, we have one in the entryway of our home. I bought it last time I visited London.

This news was quite unsettling and I needed a few moments to myself, so I herded the three colored sheep out of the house and down the front steps to graze on the lawn while I sat and gathered my thoughts. Upon some reflection, I decided if painting sheep wasn't the latest trend, it certainly should be. My three colored sheep looked quite splendid as they wandered about the yard that day. However, success of my new invention was not to be. Nobody was interested in painting their sheep and I was left with several unsold gallons of paint in the laboratory. I have not let these go to waste, though, and believe the Shockpocket estate may be the only location in England where the sheep are regularly painted. I still think they make a fine sight. At first blush, one might jump to the conclusion that I had wasted much time and effort in my experiments to create a line of paints for sheep, not only developing the paint formulas, but spending endless hours watching the tints dry. But, like many inventions, the real success of the paint research turned out to be a product of completely different nature and altogether accidental.

During the sheep paint experiments, I learned that lamb's wool is highly effective at spreading paint. Those areas in my laboratory where the freshly painted sheep had rubbed up against the walls actually looked quite nice. The application of paint was far smoother than that from a brush. And from that discovery I created a new way to apply paint to walls. I would take a square pad of lamb's wool, dip it in paint, and slide it back and forth on the wall. The paint went on smoothly and the square pads held more paint than a brush. That discovery resulted in Shockpocket's Miraculous Sheep Wool Paint Applicators. Painters love them and they have sold brilliantly. With the money we have earned selling applicators, Katherine and I have bought a fine collection of landscape paintings that feature sheep grazing in the fields.

Nobody outside of our family knew that the invention of the paint applicators was actually the result of not listening properly, but Tweak was not so lucky when she also did not listen well and made quite an embarrassing situation for herself. It seems she overheard a gathering of people in the village talking about a group in London making all sorts of ruckus about saving the crustaceans. She thought they must be protesting the popular food *escargot* and that the protestors wanted to save the snails. It just so happens that snails are one of Sherlock's favorite snacks and this resulted in several arguments within our house. Tweak painted signs that read, *Save the Snails* and marched through the village in support of the movement to save the crustaceans. Word of Tweak's protest spread and eventually reached France with the unfortunate consequence that our family was asked not to visit their country as long as Tweak protested the Escargot industry.

One day a newspaper reporter visited the Shockpocket estate to interview Tweak about her protest. Tweak related the story about a group in London that was trying to save the crustaceans and the newspaper said they would look into it, even though they had not heard anything of the kind. Only when the reporter returned were we to learn the embarrassing truth. There is indeed a group in London protesting the killing of animals, but they are trying to save the cetaceans, not the crustaceans. Cetaceans are whales, and this group did not believe they should be killed. Tweak's signs should have read, *Save the Whales*, not *Save the Snails*. To make things worse, snails are mollusks, not crustaceans. While Tweak may be brilliant in chemistry and physics, she seems to know very little about biology.

If there is a lesson to be learned by both of these events, it may be that mistakes can lead to new discoveries. On the other hand it may be that one should listen closer and pay better attention to what they hear.

The Knock Less Monster

Monday, April 4

Since the moment we decided to compete for the Victoria medal, Tweak has been determined to return to Loch Ness and find the sea serpent again. Armed with the knowledge that Nessie seems irresistibly drawn to the scent of sardine and peanut butter sandwich crusts, Tweak is confident that another expedition will yield positive results and we will finally prove that the creature of Loch Ness truly exists.

For anyone who does not know, Tweak and I first stumbled upon the serpent on Tweak's twelfth birthday. We had flown to Loch Ness in Leonardo, our seaplane, to spend the afternoon relaxing on the water. As Leonardo gently rocked on the waves, we played card games and enjoyed a birthday lunch of peanut butter and sardine sandwiches and crisps. A short time after Tweak had tossed her sandwich crusts into the water we were surprised by the appearance of a large sea serpent only a short distance from our seaplane. It appeared that the scaly beast had a most insatiable craving for peanut butter and sardine sandwich crusts and it began to swim rapidly in circles around Leonardo eating all of the scraps. Unfortunately, in all of the commotion Tweak dropped her camera overboard and we were left with no evidence that we had found the Loch Ness monster. To make things worse, the large waves that were created by the beast rocked Leonardo wildly back and forth and resulted in the seaplane sinking to the bottom of the loch.

Okay, truth be told, there was a titch more to the sinking. Some might even say it was partially my fault, what with my placing Tweak's lighted birthday candle on a ledge directly above the seaplane's fuel tank. How was I to know that a large serpent would interrupt our picnic and make large waves that would rock the plane and tip Tweak's birthday candle into the fuel oil, setting Leonardo on fire?

At any rate, that is a completely different story. Except for the part that led to our theory that the creature of Loch Ness is not able to resist the scent of peanut butter and sardine sandwiches.

For our next expedition to Loch Ness we will use that knowledge to lure Nessie once again to our craft. But this time we will take extra precautions to avoid the unfortunate events of our last foray to the loch. Instead of using a seaplane, we will make our search from a boat specially designed for the trip. No sinking plane on this expedition. And, instead of recording the events with a handheld camera dangled over the side of the boat, Tweak will capture her photos with a camera fastened inside of the vessel. No chance of dropping it overboard and losing our evidence of the beast. No indeed. This time we will be prepared.

Sherlock has designed our new craft and it is very ingenious. The boat is about twenty feet long, eight feet across at the widest point, and shaped like an oval with rounded bow and stern. Sherlock has a theory that the oval shape will cast a shadow underwater that will be similar to the serpent's own shape. He believes that the familiar outline will be less likely to frighten the shy beast away.

Into the bow of the boat, Sherlock has fabricated a large tube that descends several feet into the water. The tube has a ladder tall enough for Tweak to climb down and into an observation pod at the bottom. Even though it is rather small, the underwater space is quite comfortable with a red leather chair that faces two round, brass-rimmed windows. The glass windowpanes are bubble shaped and protrude into the water like two large eyes. From inside the pod, Tweak will have a magnificent view of the serpent in its natural habitat and will be able to take photographs of the creature from a safe and dry location with no risk of dropping her camera overboard.

After completing the basic structure of the craft, Sherlock riveted large sheets of copper over the exterior to protect the vessel and observation pod from damage should the serpent accidentally bump into us.

While Sherlock worked on the boat hull, Tweak focused on a design for the propulsion system. Conventional steam engines make a loud knocking noise as they turn the propeller shaft and we are concerned that any loud noise may frighten the creature away. Tweak decided that we will use an electric motor to turn two propellers at the back of the boat. This will be the quietest method of moving about the loch. Tweak calculated that her batteries will last several hours before recharging.

During construction we named the boat Nautilus after Jules Verne's fictional submarine. Even though we will not go completely under water like the Nautilus, sitting inside the underwater viewing port feels very much like traveling in a submersed craft. Also, Jules Verne's vessel used a form of electric motors for propulsion so the name seemed quite logical.

After some more thought, however, Tweak suggested a different name she thinks is more appropriate to our unique craft. She said the new name still sounds a little like Nautilus but she likes it more because it refers to the quiet motor that is replacing the knocking steam engine. Even better, the new name has an uncanny resemblance to the body of water where our expedition will take place - Loch Ness.

Tweak told us her suggestion for the new name and we all agreed that it is perfect. We've now christened our vessel the Knock Less.

Sunday, April 17

Before making our expedition to Loch Ness with the Knock Less, we decided to conduct a series of tests on a small lake on our estate to ensure that the boat is seaworthy. I am happy to report that the Knock Less performed brilliantly. Tweak's propulsion system makes almost no sound and we are able to glide all about the lake without startling the local ducks and geese. The view out of the submerged viewing ports is splendid. I had no idea how many fish lived in our lake before observing them from the Knock Less. They certainly have never shown up when I tried fishing there.

During the test period, the lake water turned the copper plates that cover the vessel from a bright reddish color to a dull tarnished green. As the metallic shell has dulled and colored, the bottom of the craft has taken on the eerie appearance of a sea creature's skin and blends in quite well with the sea environment. Now the resident turtles swim alongside the new creature in their home and peer into the observation pod windows. At first this was quite startling, but we have become accustomed to it and Tweak has named each of the turtles that peek in at her as she photographs them. The time for testing has finally passed and we are ready to take the Knock Less to Loch Ness. This morning we loaded the Knock

Less onto a trailer that Sherlock built specifically for the expedition. The trailer is slightly wider and longer than the boat and has a large canvas cover that completely envelops the Knock Less to hide it from prying eyes. Our mission must be kept secret until we return home and are ready to show Tweak's photographs of Nessie to the scientific community. This evening, we enjoyed a fine Sunday dinner and celebrated our coming success. Celebrating before our expedition may seem a bit presumptuous, but we know the serpent is attracted by the scent of peanut butter and sardine sandwiches. We now have a sturdy boat that should not sink. And Tweak will take photographs of Nessie safely from the observation area where she cannot drop her camera over the side of the boat. What can go wrong?

Wednesday, April 20
Earlier today, Tweak and I found ourselves dashed into the cold waters of Loch Ness when the Knock Less overturned and sank in an unfortunate accident.

Luckily, the shoreline was not too far away and we both swam in our our finest backstrokes, to the nearest beach. After emptying the water out of our boots, hats, pockets, and goggles, we sloshed our way down a small country road to a little Scottish village where we booked rooms in a tiny local inn.

As we registered at the front desk of the inn I looked at my still-dripping daughter and said, "Tweak, I do believe I have just experienced a flicker of déjà vu."

Tweak's eyes absolutely lit up as she replied, "Let me guess. The whole swimming to shore thing, then emptying water from our boots, hats, and pockets, followed by sloshing down a small country road to a little Scottish village where we booked a couple of rooms in a tiny local inn seemed oddly familiar?"

Now it was time for my eyes to light up.

"You felt it too?"

She giggled, "Of course, Daddy. But it wasn't déjà vu. On our last visit to Loch Ness we just happened to swim to the very same shore, empty the water from our clothing on the very same beach, walk down the very same small country road to the very same little Scottish village, where we checked in to the very same tiny local inn."

She paused, "But today is different. It is not my birthday, we did not just sink our seaplane Leonardo, I did not lose my favorite camera, and I do not intend to fall into a bowl of wildflower and thistle tea and turn my hair pink this evening."

Another pause. "On the other hand, it is most likely somebody's birthday today, we did just sink our new boat, the Knock Less, I did lose my second most favorite camera, and heaven only knows what will happen this evening."

Tweak swung her arms out wide and bowed in mock respect, "So, all in all, I guess it is very much the same as last time and I completely appreciate your brief feeling of déjà vu."

As usual, I was impressed with Tweak's insight. "Spot-on, Tweak. What are the odds that we should once again find Nessie and then fall into the loch and lose several of our prized possessions just as we did a little over a year ago?"

I pulled out my notebook and pencil and glanced at my pocket watch which, quite miraculously, was still keeping time, "You do realize what this means? And furthermore, what we must do straight-away?"

Tweak glanced at my watch, "Of course. Stop for afternoon tea. It's four o'clock. I'm famished. And a spot of tea and some cucumber sandwiches would be splendid."

There's my girl. "Splendid indeed," I said. "We will enjoy a brief repast whilst I jot down a few notes in my journal."

It had taken us the better part of two days to make the drive from the Shockpocket estate to Loch Ness. The large trailer and boat were awkward to maneuver on winding roads and Livingston struggled to pull the Knock Less up steep hills. It was long going, but Tweak and I passed the time talking about Nessie and how it would feel to find the serpent and win the Victoria Medal. Yesterday we reached the part of the loch where we planned to make our search and looked for a secluded beach to launch the Knock Less. It was important that no one observe the launch. If they were to see the unusual design of the boat they might guess our activities and try to follow us, and that would most assuredly scare the creature away and end the expedition. We drove along a road that meandered up one side of the loch, sometimes next to the shore and at other times a short distance away. As dusk settled over the loch, I began to think we would not find a proper launching beach before dark. Then, Tweak pointed to a small dirt side road that led through a thick stand of trees toward the water. We turned down the road and found that it led to a secluded cove with a flat beach far from curious eyes. This was where we would make our launch. We set up camp on the shore and enjoyed a pot of rabbit stew before turning in, ready for an early start.

Today, after a quick breakfast on the beach, I backed the boat trailer down to the water's edge, removed the canvas cover from the Knock Less, and proceeded to launch the boat. Once the Knock Less settled into the water, it did not look too different from any of the other boats out on the loch. The submerged viewing port was completely hidden and the exposed portion of the boat was fairly typical aside from being rounded at both bow and stern, and even that was difficult to see from a distance. We would raise no suspicions as we made our way to the same location where we last met up with Nessie.

Tweak and I climbed on board and I took hold of the steering wheel while Tweak attended to the motor. Tweak had charged the electric batteries immediately before we left the estate and the motor started perfectly. We would have enough power to cruise on the loch for several hours. The weather could not have been any better. There was only a slight breeze and small ripples on the water. As I steered the Knock Less out onto the loch, Tweak climbed down the bow tube and into her observation area.

She called up the tube. "This is brilliant. The water is crystal clear and I can see splendidly."

After a few minutes I shouted back. "I think we are back in the cove where we landed Leonardo. I will start throwing the peanut butter and sardine sandwiches into the water."

I slowed the Knock Less down to almost a stop and threw three sandwiches over the sides of the boat. Then I sat down and waited. We did not know if Nessie would come right away or even if the creature was in that area of the loch this day. I closed my eyes and had started daydreaming when I was startled by Tweak's voice. "I see it, I see it."

I shook my head and looked around at the surface of the loch but could not see anything. No serpent. No waves or ripples. Not even the sandwiches that had apparently soaked up the water and sunk. "Tweak, I don't see a thing. What are you talking about?"

"Down here. It's down here swimming next to us."

There is only room in the viewing port for one so I leaned over the side of the boat and peered into the water to see if I could spot the creature. All I could make out was a dark shadow as long as the boat and moving parallel to us at the exact same speed we were moving.

I responded to Tweak, "I think you are just seeing our shadow under the water. I have extremely good powers of observation and that is definitely not a living creature."

Then the shadow made a sudden movement and before you could say 'My goodness, I believe that is a sea serpent and it has just turned upside down', the serpent flipped itself over and started swimming next to the Knock Less with its pale white stomach facing up at the surface and its head down by the viewing room.

This behavior seemed extremely odd until it struck me what was happening. Sherlock's design had completely fooled Nessie into thinking the Knock Less was another sea serpent swimming in the loch. Nessie was mimicking its new friend by swimming upside down alongside it. This was even better than we had imagined. Tweak would be able to take several photos as the serpent swam along with us.

Suddenly the Knock Less tilted wildly to one side and then righted itself.

"Tweak, what is happening?" I shouted down the tube.

Tweak answered, "Daddy, she is so cute—she just nuzzled the viewing pod."

Another bump. Then another, and another, each one getting much stronger and tilting Knock Less alarmingly close to tipping over.

"Tweak, what is happening now?"

"I believe she thinks the Knock Less is a serpent and is upside down because it is sick. She is trying to turn us right side up.

My first thought was, *Absolutely Brilliant! The Loch Ness serpent thinks we are another serpent and is trying to help us.* Then I had a second unsettling thought. 'If the monster's upside down sick friend is our right side up healthy boat and if she turns her upside down friend right side up, then Knock Less with us inside will be upside down.'

I yelled, "Tweak, get out of the pod quick in case she turns us over."

Tweak scrambled up and out of the tube just as the serpent gave one final shove to the viewing pod and pushed it to the surface. This flipped the Knock Less completely over and threw me and Tweak into the water. Apparently, the serpent realized her mistake when the Knock Less settled upside down, tube and viewing port pointing up into the sky and exposed machinery now facing down for her to see. By the time Tweak and I regained our composure, not only had the serpent made a dive back for the bottom of the loch, but the electric motor in the Knock Less had continued to propel the boat across the loch and it was now too far away to swim to. We lost our vessel and, once again, Tweak's camera, which was attached to the window of the viewing port so that it could not be accidentally dropped overboard.

The last we saw of the Knock Less, it had propelled itself far across Loch Ness before taking on enough water to sink. Oddly enough, the tarnished green capsized boat looked remarkably like a serpent moving across the lake with the now upright observation tube and pod giving the appearance of a long neck and head. After seeing the craft sink, we made our swim to the shore and then hiked to the local inn. Tomorrow we will walk back to the hidden cove and then drive Livingston and the trailer, minus the Knock Less, back home.

But this afternoon we enjoyed our tea and cucumber sandwiches at the inn, discussed the events of the day and talked about ideas for another expedition to the loch. Tweak already had an idea for our next boat. It would be an actual submarine so there could be no way to sink. It would be shaped like the serpent again and we would attach peanut butter and sardine sandwiches to the outside to attract the creature again.

After tea, we walked across the road in front of the inn to the beach just on the other side. A path of stone steps led down to the shoreline and at the top of the steps stood a wooden sign that read WELCOME TO LOCH NESS. As we passed by it, Tweak took a piece of chalk out of her pocket and drew a sea serpent across the bottom and then added the words HOME OF NESSIE above it. I gave her a slight scowl, but then had to laugh. Now the world would know her nickname for the sea monster of Loch Ness.

We walked down the beach and sat by the water's edge to contemplate the events of the day. It was quite peaceful and we were the only ones on the shore other than a lone man wearing a long black coat and bowler hat standing behind the sign Tweak had just sketched on. He held a pair of binoculars to his eyes and seemed to be searching for something out on the loch. Neither of us spoke much as we also looked out over the large body of water, aware that the two of us knew what no others were certain of. A large creature lived beneath those waters. Not dangerous. Just shy. And with an insatiable appetite for peanut butter and sardine sandwiches.

When it was time to walk back to the inn, I looked over at the man down the beach and he appeared to be looking at us through his binoculars, but then quickly turned them back to the loch.

Later this evening, Tweak and I celebrated our success at once again finding Nessie. We still do not have any proof to show the world, but we have proved to ourselves that we know the secret of finding the creature and can find her again.

Both of us still had a chill from our swim so we ordered a hearty dinner of Shepherd's Pie with chips on the side. As we were finishing our dessert of bread pudding and custard and young man burst into the restaurant shouting, "Someone found the serpent!"

Tweak and I exchanged glances. Had someone overheard our conversation? We had been most careful to speak quietly and not let out our secret. Perhaps this was better. Now that people knew about our discovery we would not need to be so secretive. We would come back again and simply ask the locals to stay away as we searched the loch.

Another diner in the pub laughed at the young man. "Sure they did. Along with all the others that have seen the beast over the years." The others in the restaurant joined his laughter.

"No, he really did. This afternoon. And he has the photograph to prove it."

Now Tweak and I exchanged worried looks. Was it possible that her camera had broken free of the Knock Less and floated to shore where someone found it and processed the film?

"And just where did he find the creature?" another diner spoke up.

"He was on the point across the loch with a camera taking pictures of the scenery. The lucky bloke saw a large creature swimming across the loch and snapped a photograph just before it dove under the water."

Tweak and I exchanged knowing glances. That was exactly where the Knock Less cruised and sank. What an odd turn of events. Tweak and I had again found the Loch Ness monster and once again had no photos to prove it. And now a photo that people believe is of the serpent is actually of our very own boat, the Knock Less, floating across the loch before sinking to the bottom.

I was about to stand up and announce the real facts of the day when the owner of the Inn spoke up, "This is great. We will become the biggest tourist destination in Scotland. Everyone will want to come here to see the monster. We need to take some fishing boats out to trap it. Then we can keep it in an enclosed pen outside of the Inn and charge visitors to see it."

Another man shouted, "No. You have no idea how dangerous the monster could be. It should be captured, studied and then taken to a proper laboratory to be dissected."

This was not good at all. Tweak and I only wanted to prove that Nessie existed. We never intended for her to be captured or, worse yet, dissected. The crowd in the pub became more excited about the idea of capturing the serpent and Tweak and I decided it best to leave the chaotic gathering and retire to our rooms for the night.

As we walked out the front entrance, a man in a long black overcoat and bowler hat stood inside the door making notes in a small book. He resembled the man we saw earlier on the beach. I am quite certain that I heard him snicker as we passed by.

Bad News, Good News

Friday, April 22

Tweak and I arrived home today after our disappointing expedition to Loch Ness. Without the weight of the towed boat, the drive back from Scotland was faster than the trip up. But still the journey seemed to take forever. Tweak and I both had heavy hearts and did not look forward to sharing our news with Katherine and Sherlock. We spent the entire drive in silence.

My pocket watch read a little after four o'clock when we finally turned into the driveway to the Shockpocket estate. Katherine heard Livingston rumbling up the drive and ran across the lawn to welcome us home. From the empty boat trailer and our sour expressions, Katherine could tell that the expedition had not gone well. She told us to go clean up while she prepared tea and biscuits. We would then gather in the study where Tweak and I could recount our adventure.

After Tweak and I washed up and put on fresh clothes, we all gathered in the study in front of the chalk board. Katherine set out a tray of biscuits and poured us all steaming cups of Earl Grey tea as I began to describe the events that led to the sinking of the Knock Less. I explained how the boat must have looked to the serpent like one of its own kind, and how it swam along beside us for a bit. I told of how splendid it was when the serpent turned upside down and gazed directly at the observation pod as Tweak took photos through the portholes. And then I described how the serpent had mistaken the boat for another serpent in trouble and tried to right the distressed fellow creature, in the process tipping the Knock Less upside down.

As Sherlock listened to our story, he walked up to the blackboard, picked up a piece of chalk from the rail and began drawing. After I described how we tipped over, Sherley started to explain ways that he could improve the boat and make it more seaworthy. He became more and more excited as he showed us a new and improved hull design and described how it would not sink and would allow us to finally capture and bring back pictures of the Loch Ness serpent.

That's when Tweak interrupted. "Sherlock, wait. There is more to the story. We can never go back to find the serpent."

Sherlock turned toward Tweak and looked at her as though she was completely daft. "And why, little sister, do you not want to go back and get proof that you have made the greatest discovery of the year? With your photos, we will surely win the Victoria Medal."

Tweak responded. "Because someone took a photograph of the Knock Less before it sank and they think they have a photo of the real Loch Ness creature."

Sherlock replied, "How is that a problem? Now there will be more excitement about the serpent. We can tell the local villagers that we know the secret of how to find it and ask them to help pay for our new research vessel. We don't need to tell them that the photo they have is actually of our boat sinking."

Tweak looked exasperated. "No, Sherlock. Listen to me. The locals said they want to capture the beast and keep it in a pen for a tourist attraction. Even worse, one person suggested that the creature is a monster and that they must dissect and study it. "

Katherine gasped, "Oh my goodness. We never wanted to harm her."

Sherlock set the chalk down next to the blackboard and returned to his chair. After a few moments of silence Katherine spoke up. Not surprisingly, she voiced the same sentiment that Tweak and I had shared the evening after spotting Nessie.

"The fact of the serpent's existence must remain hidden. Her secret will stay with us and she will continue to be safe from those that would do her harm."

Sherlock put down the chalk, thought for a moment, and then agreed that this was indeed the only humane plan. We would not speak of Nessie again, except amongst ourselves.

This turn of events, however, created a new problem. If we could not bring back proof of the Loch Ness monster to the English Royal Society of Scientific Research and Global Exploration, then what crypto-zoological discovery could we make to win the Victoria award? Sherlock returned to the blackboard and used his sleeves to erase the beginnings of the new ship design. Then he slapped at his chalk covered sleeves sending snow-like clouds of dust downward through the shafts of light that streamed through the windows.

I stared through the falling powder at the smeared chalk marks remaining on the blackboard. The long diagonal streaks reminded me of snow covered mountain slopes and, quite unexpectedly, of my father. I never really knew my father very well. He was lost on an expedition in the Himalayan Mountains when I was a young boy of seven. My mother would tell me stories of my father's adventures and I learned about his reputation as a great explorer. As I grew up, I decided that I wanted to follow in his footsteps—at least up to the point where he disappeared.

As I gazed at the blackboard, lost in thoughts of my father—God Rest His Soul—I choked up. After a moment, my mind returned to the present and I cleared my throat. To cover up my brief lapse I mumbled that some of the floating chalk dust had gotten into my eyes and throat. Then I stood up, cleared my throat again and spoke loudly. "We should go on an expedition into the Himalayan Mountains in search of the Yeti."

Katherine responded, "Are you suggesting that we make the same search as your father was on when he was lost?"

"Yes, dear. That is precisely what I am suggesting. I think we ought to follow Reginald Shockpocket's original route for his last journey. He was certain his course would lead him to the creature and I believe it may have if he had not met with some disaster. If we are very lucky we will not only find the snow creature, but also solve the mystery of my father's disappearance."

Kate replied, "Thaddeaus, my love—what makes you think you would have any better luck than your father?"

"I should think that is obvious. I would have you, Tweak, and Sherlock with me. Three of the greatest and most innovative minds I know of. Next to mine, of course. And we would bring Nana along. She may be able to sense trails and clues that we are unable to discern."

Before Katherine could respond, Tweak began to jump up and down shouting, "Yes, yes, yes." Sherlock started scribbling a new set of notes on the blackboard and working out the details for an expedition to Nepal.

I looked to Katherine for her approval. If this was to be a family expedition, I wanted everyone's agreement that we should, indeed, take on the perilous adventure. I raised my teacup and proposed, "All who agree that we should follow in Reginald Shockpocket's path and go in search of the Yeti please join me in raising your teacups."

Sherlock, Tweak and Nana excitedly raised their cups in unison. Katherine sat motionless in her chair, pondering the proposal. Then, with a calm smile, she reached over, gently took her china teacup by the handle and raised it into the air saying, "May we all be safe and gain wonderful new knowledge on our upcoming expedition into the Himalayan mountains."

Sherlock and Tweak intertwined their arms and danced in a circle singing, "We're off to find the Yeti, we're off to find the Yeti." Nana picked up her bagpipes and began playing a celebratory tune. Shandy wagged his tail, seemingly in agreement but more likely in the hope that one of us would spill our tea or drop some crumbs that he could lap up as a treat.

What began as a gloomy return to the estate turned into a brilliant day as we now begin preparations for our mission to find the Yeti and possibly, in the process, find clues to the disappearance of my father, the explorer Reginald Shockpocket.

Saturday, April 23

This afternoon Katherine and I drove into the village to visit the shops. Both of us were in good spirits. No one outside of our immediate family knew of the failed Loch Ness expedition. If we succeeded in finding the Yeti, the Shockpocket family would be recognized as great explorers and could win the Victoria Medal. Then, perhaps people would forget our past misfortunes and see us as legitimate scientists, not just some accident-prone family.

As we visited the shops and made our purchases, several shopkeepers asked us to reveal our plans to win the Victoria Medal. Even though we would not disclose any details, they all wished us luck. It seemed that our reputation for misadventure might be in the past and a new day was on the cusp.

The day was absolutely brilliant. That is, until we walked past the corner newspaper stand. The stand attendant was placing the latest copy of the *London Times* on display. There, on the front page in large letters, the headline blared:

London Times Exclusive
Shockpocket Expedition Fails

I grabbed a copy and paid the attendant as he also noticed the headline and said he was sorry to hear that I had failed again. Katherine and I walked over to a nearby bench to sit down and read the brief article. It read:

Today, an undisclosed source informed the London Times that Thaddeaus Shockpocket recently undertook a

secret expedition to Loch Ness in search of the fabled monster that some believe exists in the waters of the loch. The source revealed that the expedition turned into a complete failure when the professor's boat capsized and sank as he and his daughter Tweak cruised across the loch in their attempt to find the serpent and win the Victoria Medal. The witness also revealed that Thaddeaus Shockpocket's upturned boat was later spotted by a local and was mistakenly identified as the monster of Loch Ness.

When told of the event, Wallace Bogglesworth stated, "This is an example of another Thaddeaus Shockpocket wild goose chase. I believe the boat most probably tipped over due to being top heavy. He should be chastised for putting his young daughter in danger."

This newspaper has not yet reached Professor Shockpocket for comment.

I set the newspaper down in disbelief. Obviously, someone had seen the boat capsize. But how did they know we were searching for the serpent? This could only mean one thing. Someone had been following us. I recalled the mysterious man with binoculars on the beach at Loch Ness who was later standing by the door of the pub as we left.

I looked over at Katherine and said, "I think someone is following us. And I think I know who hired him."

The Dolphin and the Unicorn

Saturday, April 30

Today was long and grey. It has been raining endlessly for more than a week and, to top it off, Tweak has been fighting a nasty cold that she caught when we were tossed into the frigid waters of Loch Ness. Tweak is not especially fun to be around when she has a cold. She may be strong and adventurous when she is healthy, but give her a cold and she turns into the grumpiest girl you can imagine. And whatever you are imagining, well, that is probably not half as grumpy as Tweak gets when she is under the weather.

This evening, we all gathered in the study after dinner to warm up by the big stone fireplace that devoured several large logs and gave off a sweet blend of pine scent and smoke.

Tweak sat cross-legged in her favorite spot on the hearth and pulled an old worn and frayed wool blanket over her shoulders. As she sipped at a cup of tea with a spot of honey to soothe her throat, Shandy stretched out on the hearth next to her. The big yellow dog twitched and made muffled woof sounds as he chased a rabbit in his dreams. Legs kicking, tongue hanging out—it was quite the chase and lasted several minutes before he seemed to lose interest. As suddenly as he had started, he stopped and fell back into a deep sleep.

Tweak giggled, "He is so funny when he dreams." She patted Shandy on his side and he resumed snoring before letting out a final muted woof, either in response to Tweak's touch or as one last warning to the dream rabbit.

Sherlock sat perched on the top shelf of the tall mahogany bookcase to the right of the fireplace. Seeing the young man sitting up there next to the ceiling is rather disconcerting, but since our return from Brazil, Sherlock has made a habit of spending most evenings perched at the top of the bookcase. It seems that five years of living in the Amazon jungle has led to his feeling most secure when sitting several feet off the ground. My guess is that this habit was developed to stay safe from large predatory animals at night. I know it is not due to a fear of bugs and other crawlies because Sherlock developed quite a taste for snacking on insects during his time in South America. In fact, he has maintained quite a fondness for the occasional crawly snack, and the Shockpocket estate has never been as free of insects as it is now.

Most evenings, Katherine and I sit side by side on a brown leather couch several feet back from the fire as we chat about the day's events and play a few rounds of backgammon. Tonight Katherine decided to sit in an overstuffed green velvet chair that she pulled over to the fireplace to be closer to the ailing Tweak. I took up a spot in a matching velvet chair that I also pulled closer to the fire. It seemed like a good evening to read a story to the children, so I asked if anyone had a favorite tale they would like to hear. To my surprise, neither Tweak nor Sherlock were interested in a story from any of the books in our library. In fact, they had quite a different idea for the evening.

Tweak said she and Sherley wanted to play the story game. The story game is a Shockpocket tradition where one family member brings an object to the study and then asks another family member to make up a story about the object.

Sherlock had been poking around in the attic of the Shockpocket mansion earlier in the day and uncovered an aged wooden trunk with rusty hinges and a broken lock. Not sure if he should open the trunk, his curiosity got the better of him and he lifted the heavy lid. The hinges squeaked as the trunk revealed a heap of time-worn clothing. Sherlock could tell from the clothing that the contents of the trunk were very old. He dug through the cloth to see if there were any interesting relics from the family's past. It seemed the trunk was only filled with clothes until he found, at the very bottom, a large banner with a unique design stitched onto it. He had never seen the banner or the design before and took it to Tweak to see if she knew anything about it.

The banner was about three feet tall by five feet wide. It was divided into two triangles by a diagonal grey stripe that ran from the upper right corner to the lower left corner. The upper left triangle was deep blue with an image of a dolphin jumping out of the water. The lower right area of the banner was dark green with the image of a unicorn standing on its hind legs. Tweak did not know where the flag came from but said that she had seen a similar image on the cover of an old book in the library and had always wondered what it meant. Together, Tweak and Sherlock decided it would be fun to make up a story around the images. Little did they know that the truth behind the banner was far more interesting than any story Katherine or I could make up.

Sherley unfurled the flag from his spot on top of the bookcase and announced that he and Tweak would like to hear a story about their find in the attic. As soon as Katherine saw the banner she smiled. "My-oh-my, I haven't seen that in years."

I looked at the banner and then at Tweak and Sherley, "There is no need to make up a story for this object." I said. "The real story is brilliant enough. But your mother must tell it. The banner belongs to her."

I poked at the fire and added another log as Sherley dropped the flag into Kate's lap. She laid it across her skirt and asked the children, "Are you ready?" Both Sherley and Tweak fidgeted and nodded anxiously while yellow flickers of firelight danced across the images of the dolphin and unicorn.

Katherine lowered her voice and began. "In a place long ago and a time far away, there lived a unicorn. The unicorn was the color of fresh churned cream and had a single beautiful horn of ivory that sprung from the middle of his brow. His hair was as soft as the softest silk blanket you have ever cuddled into, and his eyes were warm and comforting.

"In that time the unicorn was the noblest creature on the island of Albion. He was powerful and wise and protected all of the other animals in the forest. But he was also gentle and nurturing, and all the woodland creatures would gather around the Unicorn each day to bask in his glow.

"That is, all except humans, for man had always hunted the elusive unicorn for its magical horn. Only young maidens could approach the unicorn, and only the purest of them could touch him and remain in his magical presence. One such maiden lived in the land of Albion. She would often sneak out of her village at dusk to visit the unicorn in his clearing in the nearby forest. She would lie alongside the white beast and rest her head on his neck as the breeze blew the strands of his silky white mane across her face. There, the maiden would close her eyes and daydream of adventures in lands that lay across the sea that surrounded Albion.

"What the maiden did not know is that the Unicorn also dreamed. And his dreams were also of travel to other lands.

"One cool fall evening, the young maiden went to bed early as she had been troubled by a cold for the past several days. She tossed and turned with a fever until after midnight when she decided to slip out of the house and go into the woods to find the unicorn. She hoped his presence would remove her fever and make her better.

"The maiden hiked to the clearing where she normally visited the unicorn but he was nowhere to be seen. She stilled her breath and listened carefully, hoping to catch the sound of the unicorn walking through the brush. Instead, she heard noises she did not recognize. They seemed to be coming from a stand of trees that stood by the edge of the sea.

"The maiden was a little frightened by these sounds, but her curiosity got the better of her. She crept as quietly as possible to the far side of the woods. There she hid behind a large oak tree and looked out over the beach to see what was making the sounds that filled that air. To her surprise, there in the moonlight she saw the beautiful white unicorn prancing along the sea's edge. In the ocean, a short distance from shore, a glistening grey dolphin danced on the waves. Every so often the dolphin made a loud clicking noise followed by chirping sounds, and in return the unicorn would rise up on his rear legs and let out a baying sound. As the maiden listened more closely, the clicks and chirps and baying began to sound like music.

"Her curiosity grew stronger and she crawled as quietly as she could onto the beach to better see the dance and hear the music of the dolphin and the unicorn. The maiden lay very still so as not to be detected by the creatures. Suddenly, the unicorn turned and faced the young maiden. She was frightened, for what she had observed must truly be some secret magic that was not to be seen by mortal beings. The unicorn rose up on his hind legs and bayed before he galloped at full speed directly towards the young maiden, kicking up a spray of sand as his hooves pounded across the shore. The maiden covered her eyes fearing that the white beast would trample her. But instead, when the unicorn reached the maiden he pulled up to a stop and then dropped down onto his front knees as if bowing to the girl. Then he gently touched his horn to her head and the maiden's fever disappeared. As the great white beast stood up, he swung his head toward the water's edge as if summoning the maiden to follow him.

"If any one of us had observed that night's events, they would have witnessed the most miraculous of sights. There, at the edge of the great sea, three moonlit creatures sang and danced together in the shallow waters. A white unicorn spinning, prancing and rising up on his hind legs as if to claw at the stars in the night sky. A glistening dolphin doing flips in the waves and dancing on her tail. And a young maiden in fluttering nightdress, twirling and skipping across the sea foam as she splashed her hands in the tide. Later, in the middle of the night, the unicorn escorted the young maiden home where she changed into a dry nightdress, climbed into her cozy bed, and slept the deepest sleep a young maiden could.

"In the days that followed, the unicorn let the maiden join in his nightly dance with the dolphin. Each night the unicorn would prance a little further into the water and get closer to the dolphin until, one night, the unicorn left the beach and swam out into the sea to the dolphin. The two creatures seemed to celebrate even more as they moved in circles around each other, clicking, chirping and baying. To the maiden, their songs sounded even more beautiful as the melodies merged harmoniously. The maiden could tell the dolphin and the unicorn had become the closest of friends—this creature of the land and being of the sea—and she sensed that soon the unicorn would leave the land to be with his friend for all time.

"Each night the three would dance in the water and the dolphin and unicorn would swim further out from the shore. Then, on a night with a full harvest moon, the three danced and sang for what seemed like hours. Longer than they ever had before. It was as if this night was different than all the others and the three magical creatures did not want the evening to end. The young maiden splashed in the waves and the dolphin and unicorn swam and sang together farther and farther out to sea.

"Finally, as quickly as it had started, the dancing stopped. The water became still and all became quiet. The maiden looked out at the black sea, which was now a calm surface with only the rippling image of the moon dancing on top, and she knew the unicorn had left to be with his love.

"Now, you will find many that say unicorns never existed and that they are simply a myth. But our family knows the secret of the unicorn. They have not existed in ages. That is true. But they did live at one time and the last unicorn was the great white unicorn of Albion who left the land for his love in the sea. There is even proof—if you know where to look for it.

"For when the great white unicorn of Albion and the noble grey dolphin of the sea traveled the world together, they had children. Today you can even see their descendants. They are the white narwhales that roam the northern oceans of the world. With their white dolphin-like bodies and long unicorn horns the narwhales remind our family that love crosses boundaries, creates beautiful futures, and gives us memories of magical pasts."

Katherine touched the dolphin and unicorn figures on the banner. Both Sherlock and Tweak had drifted off to sleep, but I think they were dreaming of maidens and unicorns, of dolphins and narwhales, and of all the distant lands they have seen and have yet to explore.

Finally, Katherine read the embroidered words on a small scrap of cloth sewn to the backside of the banner. It is said that they were originally written by the maiden of the unicorn, a long ago ancestor of Katherine.

Common threads tie us together.

Whim and whimsy to free our soul.

Travel with me to the ends of the earth.

Together forever, not separate, but whole.

My dearest Kate looked at me with a warm smile. "I would say that describes our family quite nicely, wouldn't you?"

I nodded.

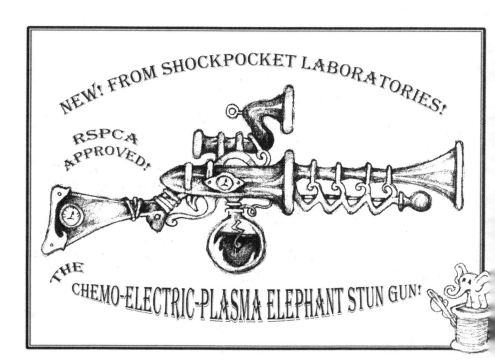

Chemo Electric Plasma Elephant Stun Gun

Thursday, May 12

The Chemo Electric Plasma Elephant Stun Gun may just be the most advanced invention I have developed. Last year, when Tweak and I invented the buried catapult device for relocating nuisance rabbits from our garden to neighboring properties, we were pleasantly surprised to be recognized by the Royal Society for Prevention of Cruelty to Animals for creating a safe and efficient way to relocate problem animals. They were impressed with our method of sending the little pests across great distances through the air and then catching them unharmed in nets at a target location. This led to us create S.H.A.R.E.—Shockpocket's Humane Aerial Relocation Enterprises—and was the beginning of a brilliant working relationship between the Shockpockets, the RSPCA and the local zoo.

Upon presenting us the certificate for achievement, a representative of the society, Officer Clive A. Trapman, asked if we could modify our device to relocate animals other than rabbits. In particular, he wished us to set up catapults to deal with a pair of giraffes that had the nasty habit of regularly escaping the town zoo and walking some distance to a neighboring village where they would munch on the thatch roof of one particular home. While launching rabbits was enough of a challenge, what with needing to calculate their flight path and compensating for the RED or (Rabbit Ear Drag factor, the challenge of launching animals such as giraffes was much greater. Not only was there the ever so problematic LND (Long Neck Drag factor), but the effect of their gangly legs in flight would also need to be accounted for. We could easily catapult small animals such as turtles and squirrels with our devices but struggled to come up with a system that could launch and catch larger animals without undue harm.

While Tweak and I were working on the various designs for a larger aerial relocation device, the head zoo keeper approached us about helping him solve another dilemma. It seems that most animals do not appreciate visits from the zoo veterinarian when it is time for their physicals and shots. As often as not, a visit from the veterinarian leads to a wild chase. As soon as an animal spots the man who only visits when he wants to poke and probe said animal, it runs all around its enclosure while being chased by a dozen frantic zoo helpers carrying large nets. After these chases, the helpers are tired, the veterinarian is exhausted, and the animal is in an exceptionally unpleasant mood. This is especially bad when the animal being chased is a lion that has now decided it wants to take a bite of anyone who approaches it.

The chief zookeeper thought it would be brilliant if we could invent a device that would make it easier to catch the animals without frightening them or making them angry. I suggested that the veterinarian dress up in a costume to look like whatever animal he was trying to examine. The zookeeper said they had tried that plan in the past and would not be doing it again. He would not tell me what had happened and seemed agitated when I asked.

I gave this new challenge much thought and decided that the best course would be to create a device that puts an animal to sleep for a few minutes while the veterinarian performs his examination and gives the animal its shots. This has led to the creation of the Chemo Electric Plasma Elephant Stun Gun. Since the introduction of this amazing device, the veterinarian has been able to examine all of the zoo inhabitants with nary an accident or agitated animal. Some have asked why I set out to develop an Elephant Stun Gun instead of an all-animal stun gun. That is a valid question and many have guessed that developing a gun to stun an elephant into sleep makes complete sense because an elephant is a very large creature and if the device can put an elephant to sleep, it will most certainly give any other animal a decent nap. That guess is very logical. It is wrong, but still logical. Actually, it is simply a coincidence that the stun gun was originally designed to work on an elephant. You could even say it was a matter of convenience. In fact, the Chemo Electric Plasma Stun Gun works on all animals but I continue to call it the Chemo Electric Plasma Elephant Stun Gun in honor of the test subject that I used while perfecting the final design.

Let me explain. Many years ago, Katherine, Sherlock and I spent a brilliant two-week holiday on an elephant caravan in the Serengeti to celebrate Sherlock's fourth birthday. During the expedition, Sherlock had the opportunity to become friends with a baby elephant that had joined its mother on the journey. Each day, the caravan would travel a short distance to a new campsite and there we would spend the afternoon and evening observing the landscape and local wildlife. Sherlock and the young elephant would scamper about the camp, running between the tents and playing until they were both exhausted. Then the two would curl up together on the ground next to our tent, Sherlock lying on his back with his head resting on the baby elephant's side and the little elephant resting her trunk across his chest. As the days passed, the two little ones became inseparable and it was clear that they had formed a special friendship. Katherine and I were happy that the expedition and Sherlock's birthday had gone well, but neither of us looked forward to the end of the holiday. We wondered how Sherlock would handle leaving his new companion.

Then, a most miraculous thing happened. On the last evening of the expedition, the leader of the caravan asked me to join him in his tent for a private discussion. I was certain that he was irritated about the bond that had developed between the elephant and Sherlock. Surely, by becoming so close to an outsider, the elephant would be more difficult to train for its work duties as it grew older. I was prepared to listen to an angry lecture and, perhaps, be asked to compensate him for ruining one of his elephants. But to my complete surprise he was quite pleased with the friendship that had developed between the elephant and my son. It seems that the baby elephant was a runt and would never grow up to be as large and strong as the other elephants. In fact, she would be of no practical use to him at all as an adult elephant and would only be a burden for the caravan to take care of. He had planned to look for a zoo that would take her but did not like the idea of the little elephant spending the rest of her life in a pen. But now, seeing the happiness the elephant brought to Sherlock, he thought I might be interested in taking the young animal back to our estate in England where we could take care of her and give her space to roam.

I said I would discuss it with Katherine, even though I already knew her response would be positive. We have plenty of space on the estate and creating shelter and roaming space for the small elephant would not be a problem. The next morning we told Sherlock that we were taking his new friend home with us. He exclaimed that this was the best birthday he had ever had and promptly named his new friend Lucy. To this day, we have no idea why Sherlock chose the name Lucy, but it is a fine name and she has been a member of the family since.

That brings us back to the present and why the stun gun is called an *elephant* stun gun. As I developed the chemo electric plasma stun gun, I needed a large animal on which to test its effectiveness. I thought it was most reasonable that Lucy be my test subject. First, she is located conveniently on the Shockpocket estate so I did not need to travel to test the gun. Second, the plasma ray is designed to instantly and painlessly place any animal small or large into a deep sleep for a few minutes, and Lucy is indeed a large animal. She may be small for a typical elephant, but she was a better choice for the tests than Shandy or Nana. And third, the trials with Lucy would not harm her. They would simply provide her with a few unexpected naps. And what animal doesn't like the occasional nap? The reason the device is called the Chemo Electric Plasma Elephant Stun Gun is to recognize Lucy's role in the development of the gun. And it sounds better than Chemo Electric Plasma Lucy Stun Gun.

I have also been asked how the stun gun works. Well, it is quite complicated and I am not quite sure I can clearly explain the device. Suffice it to say that I use a carefully regulated combination of chemicals that are then electrified. The resulting reaction generates a plasma beam that exits through a focusing lens mounted on the front of the gun. When the beam strikes an animal it interacts with the molecules of the creature and immediately puts it to sleep. Then, a short time later, the target subject wakes up completely unharmed. To be honest, there were a few accidents during its development that have led me to prevent others from using the device. Fortunately, most of the mishaps occurred before I tested the gun on Lucy. I prefer not to think of the consequences had they occurred with an actual animal. It was rather a challenge to test an animal sleeping device on plants but I found that my Venus Flytraps made worthy test subjects. I only exploded a few of them before I perfected the electrochemical mixture and could stun the plants harmlessly before they woke up and devoured the flies I had placed on them.

The only mishap I had with Lucy actually led to another invention. During one of my tests I discovered that if you hook the electric wires on the gun in a backward fashion the Chemo Electric Plasma Elephant Stun Gun becomes a Chemo Electric Plasma Elephant Shrinky Ray Gun. While Lucy is not exactly large to begin with, I do not think she appreciated being the size of a corgi dog for several days after one such incident. Worse yet (and I hesitate to share this), on the day I accidentally shrunk Lucy, Katherine had been observing me from behind without my knowing. At the sight of Lucy shrinking, Kate screamed and I spun around, startled. My finger accidentally depressed the stun gun trigger as I faced Katherine and she was also miniaturized. Both Lucy and Katherine returned to normal size in a few days and I think it all turned out rather brilliantly, what with discovering how to make the stun gun into a shrinky ray gun.

This completely solved the animal relocation catapult dilemma. We can now use the Chemo Electric Plasma Shrinky Ray Gun to shrink large animals before launching them with the catapult. On the other hand, Lucy now tends to run from me whenever she sees the stun gun. And to this day Katherine refuses to see the humor in my calling her Tinkerbelle during her wee time, or saying that she should only be a "teensy" angry.

Kathmandu

Monday, May 16

Preparations for the Yeti expedition are going splendidly. For this journey we will travel light, as there is no need for bulky scientific apparatus. Other than warm clothing, maps, sextant, compass, and chemo electric plasma elephant stun gun, no extra equipment will be required. We will use the journals and original expedition plan of the late Reginald Shockpocket to retrace his route into the Himalayas. Once there, we will undertake our own effort to find the elusive Yeti.

I am considering using our airship, ALBION 77, to transport us to each of Reginald's planned stops along the route to Nepal. It sustained only minor damage when it made an unplanned and rather rapid landing in Brazil late last year. When Tweak and I made our journey to the Amazon Basin in August to join Katherine and Sherlock and check the airworthiness of the crashed airship, I brought along patches for the moth

holes that had led to its descent, and a helium genera-
tor to re-inflate the balloons. The patches held and we
were able to fly ALBION 77 back to England where I
fabricated new balloons to replace those damaged by
the ravenous Brazilian moths. I also made a thorough
inspection of the ship's mechanical systems to ensure
that all airship controls were installed properly. We do
not want a repeat of the airship runaway incident that
took Kate from us last time.

I am also pondering the idea of using the shrink version of the plasma gun to miniaturize Lucy and bring
her along on the expedition. Once we land in Nepal she
would return to normal size and could carry our gear—
and each of us from time to time—to give our legs a rest.

Saturday, May 21

At today's family meeting, I mentioned the idea of
shrinking Lucy and bringing her along on the trip.
Katherine reacted by simply frowning silently. Sherlock drew two pictures on the blackboard. The first
chalk drawing showed ALBION 77 flying high above the
ground with a little elephant peeking out through the
railing on the deck. The second sketch showed ALBION
77 falling out of the sky with a full size elephant on the
deck, legs poking out through broken deck railings on
both sides of the ship. Tweak simply giggled and Nana
signed a joke that I will not repeat.

Upon further reflection, I have decided to abandon
the miniaturized elephant idea. This is probably for the

best as, truth-be-told, I never really know how long the shrink effect will last. Two weeks ago I miniaturized one of our sheep and expected it to return to normal size within a few hours. It is still only one inch tall and currently lives inside a tiny barn Sherlock built for it. If we were to take Lucy on the expedition, she might return to normal size while we are in flight resulting in another ALBION 77 crash-landing. Or she might stay tiny during the entire expedition and we would need to carry her instead of the other way around.

Later today, I further decided that we will not even fly to Nepal in ALBION 77. Instead, we will take our truck, which we call Livingston. Even though the airship is certainly the most comfortable way to travel and would shorten the time required to travel to Nepal, I now believe that taking the land route is more practical and will allow us to follow the exact path originally taken by Reginald Shockpocket. I think it is possible that he never made it to Nepal, so traveling on the roads he took may lead us to clues about his disappearance. Tomorrow we begin packing our supplies and loading them into Livingston. In five days we will set out for Kathmandu.

Tuesday, June 21

We have completed our long journey to Kathmandu. It has taken the better part of four weeks to make the drive, but we have been fortunate to have clear weather and good roads along the route described in Reginald's expedition plan. Wherever possible, we have spent our nights at the inns indicated in his notes. At each stop, the innkeepers have been gracious and permitted us to look at their registration records to see if Reginald had signed in to their lodgings when he was passing through. To our delight, we have found his signature in all of the registration books. This confirms that he followed his planned route and made it to each stop along the way. At a couple of the inns, the keepers even remembered him. It seems that Reginald made quite an impression as he told stories of his great expeditions and how he was on his way to the Himalayas in pursuit of the Yeti.

This afternoon we checked into the inn listed for Reginald's stay in Kathmandu. It is here where we will rest up before driving as far as Livingston will take us into the mountains and then making the rest of our trek on foot. I asked the innkeeper if we could look through some of his old registration logs. As with the other inns, we were granted permission to search for Reginald's signature. Once again, his signature was in the book on the exact date that he had planned to be there. It appears that his expedition had gone according to plan up to this point. I scanned further down the pages to see if I could spot another signature. His original plan would have put him back at the inn three weeks after his departure into the mountains. There was no sign that Reginald had checked back into the inn.

I explained to the innkeeper the reason for my curiosity and he suggested I look in the inn's guest book. It is customary for travelers to leave messages in the guest book as they check out, typically complimenting the inn on its accommodations or praising the local environs for their beauty. Perhaps Reginald had left a note or message that would help in our search. He walked over to a filing cabinet buried under an assortment of cleaning supplies in the back corner of the room. It was clear that no one had looked in its drawers in many years. After several minutes of rummaging through the files, the innkeeper pulled out the guest book from thirty-four years ago and carried it over to the counter. He flipped through the yellowed pages until he came to the date of Reginald's departure into the mountains.

At the very top of the page was Reginald's handwriting.

Thank you so much for the wonderful stay. I would highly recommend your fine inn to any who wish to pass through Nepal. Now I am off in search of the Yeti. If all goes as planned, I will be checking back into your inn within the next three weeks with proof that the Yeti exists. Wish me luck. Reginald Shockpocket.

I looked through the guest book for additional entries by Reginald, but there were none. It appears that he never made it back to the inn. Two days later we set out on the final leg of our expedition into the mountains. I do not know if we will find the Yeti or Reginald. I just hope we find more clues to his disappearance. I now find myself more interested in solving my father's disappearance than finding the snow creature.

Yeti

Saturday, June 25

Yesterday morning we left Kathmandu and drove a good distance into the mountains before having to park Livingston due to rough terrain. We spent last night camped by the truck and set out this morning for what we hoped would be a day of discovery. According to Reginald's map, he believed the Yeti could be found within a day's hike from where we left Livingston. With high spirits, we set out upon the hillside of dark barren rock and blinding white snow. Thank goodness Sherlock has designed special goggles to prevent snow blindness. The brass goggles have colored lenses that may be changed according to the light. Dark grey for the bright sun of day, clear for dusk, and yellow for foggy conditions. In addition to the colored lenses, the goggles are equipped with additional lenses that swivel down to create magnifying lenses for examining small specimens, or telescopic lenses to observe objects from a great distance. Sherlock also fabricated spiked plates that strap onto our boots so that we do not slip as we walk across the ice fields. We made good time today and have arrived in the general area where Reginald indicated the Yeti may be found. Late this afternoon we had the good fortune to find a cave that will make the perfect shelter and location for our base camp. In here, we are shielded from any wind or inclement weather that may pass through. The cave is the size of a large room and has plenty of space for us to cook meals and sleep. A low and narrow passageway leads off from the main. Perhaps tomorrow I will explore the tunnel to see if there is anything of interest.

Tonight we built a roaring fire in our temporary home and settled in for a hearty feast of lamb stew and biscuits. Nana provided the evening entertainment. First, she regaled us with several fine melodies on the bagpipe. I am certain the wondrous sounds of the pipes carried across the snowfields and mountainsides entrancing all who heard the sweet harmony.

When she had finished her energetic recital, Nana continued to entertain us by signing jokes while also voicing them in her chimp dialect. We understand nothing of her language but all in our family are well versed in the sign language that we taught her when we brought the orphaned chimp home from Africa several years ago.

The only difficulty comes when Nana is especially excited and begins to either sign so fast that we cannot keep up, or when she simply forgets to sign all of the words in a joke. This leads to some stories merging into others to create a number of interesting and often confusing punchlines.

For instance,

Question: Why did the chicken cross the road:

Answer: Because canvas is scratchy.

Clearly, Nana had combined the *Why did the chicken cross the road* joke with the *Why was the Frenchman dabbing his eye with a silk hanky* joke. Anyway, as Nana was telling her jokes this evening, we all rolled on the cave floor in laughter at both the good jokes and the bad. Katherine's giggles sounded like bells echoing off the cave walls, Tweak shrieked and Sherlock snorted. The chorus of laughter was rounded out with my chortling plus the indescribable sound of chimp snickering.

Only after a while did it dawn on me that Nana was telling the punchline to one of her stories at the very same time that we could hear chimp laughter. I waved my hands for everyone to be quiet and the cave went totally silent except for what sounded like chimp laughter coming from the side passage. The tittering continued for a moment, and then from the dark recess came a noise that can only be described as some animal version of *oops*, then silence. I looked at Nana and she shrugged her shoulders. She was as confused as we were.

Shortly after the animal sounds stopped, we began to hear footsteps coming from deep within the same dark recess. The steps were slow and each step was accompanied by the sound of something being dragged across the cave floor.

Now we became concerned. Whatever was making the footsteps was definitely making its way slowly toward us from somewhere deep within the cave. It seemed that the steps had been making their way toward us for quite some time. We wondered when the beast would reach us. Then, much to our bewilderment and terror, into the firelight stepped the Yeti. The creature was covered in light brown fur and walked awkwardly, as though it was injured or sick. It was not nearly as large as I had imagined and really not very frightening at all as it stood there staring at us. Nobody moved as we stared at the hairy animal and it stared back at us. The chemo electric plasma stun gun was packed in a box that lay across the room and was too far to reach without possibly angering the beast and triggering an attack.

As the Yeti stood at the edge of the room and studied us, it seemed to be mostly interested in Nana and gazed at her, cocking its head back and forth. I hoped it was not sizing up our dear friend for a snack. Suddenly, it made a sound that I took to be some sort of communication. I had expected that a Yeti would make frightening guttural noises and wave its arms, but instead this creature stood quite still and communicated with a voice that sounded like Nana's.

Nana appeared to be shocked by what she heard and began behaving as I have never seen, jumping up and down and spinning in circles, all the while chattering up a storm. Then she ran across the cave straight at the Yeti. Now I was even more confused. The creature said something else to Nana and she started pulling at its fur. At first I thought it had made her angry but then realized that the fur was, in fact, not that of the creature's, but was instead a coat from which stepped an adult chimpanzee that had an uncanny resemblance to Nana.

Nana turned and signed to us: "My dear human family, I would like to introduce one of my uncles from my birth home."

I can't really say what my emotions are right now. Relief that we were not confronted by the real Yeti and faced with certain death? Disappointment that we had not found the real Yeti? Or confusion as to why one of Nana's relatives was in the Himalayan Mountains hiding in a cave and dressed like a Yeti?

Sunday, June 26

Last evening we fell asleep to the sound of Nana and her uncle chattering non-stop into the wee hours of the morning. Nana was so excited at meeting her uncle that she did not take the time to sign their conversation to us. We had to wait until today to learn the story of Nana's uncle and how he came to be here in Nepal.

This morning, over a breakfast of hearty oatmeal and Masala Chai tea, Nana recounted the journey of her uncle. She had never met him before but had heard stories about her father's brother. For many years, men had come to the forest where Nana and her family lived to trap chimpanzees and ship them to zoos in other parts of the world. Whenever the hunters came, the chimpanzees would try to escape but some were always captured. That is how Nana lost her parents and became the orphan that wandered into our camp when we were in that region studying flowers for new medicines. According to the stories that her parents had told before they were taken away, Nana's father had a brother who decided to leave his home forest to search for a safer place to live. One day he announced to the others that he was going to walk until he found a place where chimpanzees were not hunted. Once there, he would live out his days without fear of capture. He left the forest and was never seen or heard of again.

According to Nana's uncle, he kept traveling from Africa, through the Middle East, and all the way to the Himalayan Mountains. Along the way, every time he thought he had found a safe new home, humans would find him and try to capture him. As he had continued to travel north and into the mountains, he became cold and thought he would need to turn back. Then he found this cave and in it the fur skin of a bear. The cave made a nice home and the fur coat kept him warm and comfortable. He also found that the humans in this region seemed to be frightened of him when he wore his coat. If he stood just right and waved his arms at humans in the distance, instead of chasing him they would scream and run away. Then he could walk into their camps and help himself to their food. Between taking foodstuffs from travelers on the mountain trails and hiking into nearby villages at night to find food left outside, he was able to make quite a comfortable home in his cave.

When Nana had finished telling her uncle's story, I asked if she thought her uncle was the Yeti of myth.

Sherlock spoke up before Nana could answer. He pointed out that the chimpanzee could not be the Yeti because the legend goes back long before Nana's uncle made his journey to the Himalayas. In fact, even Reginald's expedition would have been made before her uncle found his way to the mountain cave. Nana agreed with Sherlock and turned to her uncle to ask him if he had ever seen any other large creatures wandering in the mountains. She explained to him about the legend of the Yeti and he started laughing.

Nana signed that her uncle thinks the local people must believe he is the Yeti and that is why they run from him. He says it now makes more sense that some even leave food out for him at night.

Nana's uncle thought a bit and finally said something to Nana. She signed to us that he had never seen or heard any other creatures in this part of the mountains, only humans that would occasionally wander part way up the mountain until he screamed at them and waved his arms in the air. None have ever come close since he lived there. But he thought some humans may have camped in the cave long before he moved in. He said there were some things in the very back of the cave that looked similar to those that we carried with us.

As Nana finished signing, I practically dropped my oatmeal into the fire. "Nana, are you saying there are human articles in the back of the cave?"

Nana signed: "Yes, I believe that is exactly what I am saying. That is where he found the fur coat."

Katherine looked at me and said, "Thaddeaus, don't get your hopes up. It would be too much of a coincidence."

I grabbed a torch and started walking into the dark recess from which Nana's uncle emerged last evening. The others followed closely. The black alcove led to a small tunnel that sloped gradually downward away from the main room. As the passageway progressed, it became quite low and narrow until I could barely fit through the tight space. Then, about twenty feet into the tunnel, it made a sharp turn to the right and opened into another large chamber.

Reginald Shockpocket

Sunday, June 26 (continued)

As we entered the room-like chamber, our torches illuminated what looked like the camp of a previous expedition. A heavy layer of dust covered the equipment, indicating that it had been undisturbed for several decades. An old backpack leaned against the far wall. Not far from the backpack a sleeping bag lay unrolled on the floor. Nearby was a small portable cooking stove with a tea kettle on one of the unlit burners.

I blew some of the dust off of the backpack and lifted the canvas cover to see if the contents would provide a clue to its owners or the purpose of their expedition. Inside, the pack was stuffed with clothing but no clues as to who owned the contents. Then I found an outside pocket, and in it a journal. Katherine, Sherlock and Tweak pointed their torches at the remarkably well-preserved leather notebook. I untied the cord that held the notebook closed and opened it to the first page.

There, in handwriting that looked remarkably similar to mine, the notes read, *Expedition to the Himalayan Mountains in search of the Yeti. By Reginald Shockpocket.* I fell to my knees upon reading the words. After all these years, I could practically feel my father's presence as I held his notebook.

When I regained my composure, we gathered up the contents of the back room and carried them back to the main cave where we could examine them in better light. From the entries in Reginald's journals, it was clear that he had made the trip from England to Nepal with no setbacks. He had stayed in Kathmandu at the same inn where we had rested before making the final push into the mountains. It appeared that he had been camping in the cave for about two weeks before his journal entries stopped.

Below are some excerpts from Reginald's Journal.

<u>Base camp- Day one</u> – Today I found shelter in a cave high on the mountainside near a broad snowfield. The cavern is quite large and will make a fine location to set up the base camp for my studies.

<u>Base camp – Day two</u> – It is only the second day of my search for the Yeti and I am pleased to report that I have already found animal tracks in the snow not too far away from the cave. The sun has melted the tracks making them difficult to identify.

THADDEAUS SHOCKPOCKET: VICTORIA

<u>Base camp – Day three</u> – Today I found more tracks, these closer to the camp. The pattern of the tracks is unlike any I have encountered in the past. The creature appears to walk on four legs for a distance and then upright on two legs for stretches of time. Tonight I could distinctly hear an animal howling somewhere in the distance. I dare not go out after dark. If this is the Yeti, to do so will surely invite disaster.

<u>Base camp – Day four</u> – More tracks, nearer to the cave. It seems the creature is coming closer, perhaps working up its courage to confront me. Tonight the howls are louder. I have moved my equipment and sleeping bag into another room that I discovered beyond a narrow passage at the back of the main cave. I do not think a large creature can fit through the passage. I have also placed empty food tins at the cave entrance to alarm me should the beast enter the main cave. I think I will not sleep well tonight.

<u>Base camp – Day five</u> – Tonight I found the snow beast. Or, more accurately, it found me. Shortly after dark this evening, the howls began again. This time they were quite close and clearly moving closer. I was certain that the beast was coming to the cave so I positioned myself in the narrow passage where I had a view of the large cavern area. As I expected, the beast entered the cave, loudly sniffing as if to detect my presence. It spotted me and rose up on two legs, letting out a howl as it did. At first, I thought that the beast was indeed the Yeti so I stayed pro-

tected in the passageway. But then, the creature lay down and raised its right front leg into the air. It was then I realized that the howling creature was a large bear, possibly injured. An injured wild animal can be even more dangerous than a healthy one, but this one appeared to be quite docile. I carefully approached the beast and it simply whimpered and held its leg in the air. It appears that the bear broke its left leg some time ago and the break had healed in a crooked fashion. Walking on it must cause great pain and that has forced the animal to walk much of the time on only its back two legs. The poor beast walking upright and howling in pain is most likely what has been mistaken for a snow creature. This evening I shared my supper with the bear and he has now dozed off to sleep. I do not know what tomorrow will bring, but for tonight I think I am safe.

<u>Base camp – Day six</u> – Today, the bear slept for most of the day, snoring softly. He seems comfortable here and I think the cave may have been his home before I set up camp in it. I examined the bear closely while he slept and he appears to be quite old. I would be surprised if he has many more years left. He finally awoke late this afternoon and seems to have accepted me into his home. He made no attempts to stand today and let me share more of my food with him as he lay in the center of the room. Shortly after eating, he returned to a deep sleep. Tonight, there have been no howls out on the moonlit snowfields, only soft snoring from the bear in the main

cave. I am now almost certain that the poor beast sleeping at my side is responsible for at least some of the Yeti sightings.

Base camp – Day seven – This morning I awoke to a quiet cave. During the night, the old bear took his last breath. I am sad for his death but also happy for the beast. He will no longer suffer from his broken leg. I have decided that I will use his fur coat to make a blanket for future expeditions.

Base camp – Day nine – There are no new tracks on the nearby snowfields and the nights have been quiet since the bear entered the cave. I believe this expedition is coming to an end. I will continue to search for two more days and then return to Kathmandu.

Base camp – Day ten – This evening, I was awakened by new howling from the moonlit fields. The new howls are distinctly different than those made by the bear and appear to be coming from the other side of a nearby ridge. Tomorrow I will rise early and embark on a day trek into the next valley to investigate further. Could this be the real Yeti?

Following this last journal entry, the pages were blank. It would seem that Reginald set off to the next valley and never returned. Perhaps he found the Yeti and met an untimely end. Tomorrow we will make our way over the ridge to see what lies beyond.

The Valley

Monday, June 27

This morning we left the cave and climbed up the mountain to the narrow exposed rock ridge that sits far above our camp. The trek went rather quickly and we found ourselves looking down into the adjacent valley only three hours after we left the cave. The sharp ridge is really quite narrow along its top edge and barely large enough to stand on. From our viewpoint on the ridge we could see a small village at the bottom of the valley. Next to the village runs a small river that churns with the white waters of snow and glacier run-off. There do not appear to be any roads leading into or out of the village, only a few trails that follow the river. My guess is that one of the trails leads to Kathmandu. The snow slope down to the village is wide and smooth and perfect to test out the skis we had packed. This would be the first time any of us had used skis and I hoped we would make the descent without incident.

Katherine started first and slid across the snow field to one edge. Once there, she sat down, lifted the skis into the air and turned them to face the opposite direction. Then she stood up and skied across the field in the opposite direction. The method seemed very safe but it would take her hours to reach the bottom.

Sherlock started next and used a skiing technique similar to Katherine's, but different. Instead of sitting and lifting his skis to face the opposite direction, Sherlock stayed on his feet as he turned to face the opposite direction.

Tweak would have none of that and said she would turn her skis while sliding down the hill. She pushed off and headed for the side of the snowfield, but her path aimed farther down the hill. As she approached the edge of the snowfield, she hopped into the air several times, each time turning the skis until at last she was facing the opposite side of the snow field. Soon, she was making smooth turns on the pristine snow as though she had been skiing her entire life.

Once I was certain the rest were proceeding safely, I pushed off from the top of the ridge. I chose Tweak's technique. It looked easy enough and would allow me to make fewer turns and reach the bottom of the hill faster. Also, I had secretly applied a layer of wax to the bottom of my skis to speed my descent. I'd been experimenting with coatings that would make skis slide better. If my combination of paraffin wax and bacon grease worked as expected, I would have a new product, Shockpockets Miracle Ski Wax. The formula worked well in my laboratory tests and made the bottoms of the skis quite slippery. The only problem I encountered was Shandy's habit of licking off the bacon wax. But that would be no problem. If the wax succeeded in making the skis faster, I would simply use one of my smell modification formulas to mask the bacon odor.

As soon as I set out, it became apparent there was a problem with my skis. I copied Tweaks technique each time I tried to turn. I waved my arms, screamed, and turned my body in the direction I wished to head. But instead of turning, the skis only pointed straight down the hill and slid faster and faster—straight for the river at the bottom of the valley, and the village on the far side.

The good news is that the skis were amazingly fast and by going straight down I reached the village in no time at all. Unfortunately, once at the bottom of the hill, I had no idea how to stop. I was traveling at such a speed that when I reached the river I flew straight across the rushing waters and up the far bank. The village was a blur as I sped through the main square and up the opposite hillside before being brought to an abrupt stop by a large Yak in my path. The Yak let out one loud howl as I collided with it, but then seemed none the worse as it walked away with my pith helmet hanging off one of its horns. It glanced back at me and made disapproving grunts.

I, on the other hand, was a bit shaken. After removing a ball of Yak fur from my mouth and untying the leather straps that held the skis to my feet, I limped back down the hill and into the village just as Tweak was crossing the bridge into the main square. Sherlock and Katherine had copied Tweak's skiing technique and made their way across the bridge a short time later. Fortunately, none of them had witnessed my accident, but they were all curious about the clumps of Yak fur hanging off my clothes. I simply told them that I had run into a friendly Yak in the village and that it had shed on me while I was admiring its soft fur.

By now, several villagers had gathered in the square to see what all of the ruckus was about. Most of the residents here do not speak English but one of them stepped forward and, in perfect English, introduced himself as a local guide. He explained that he spent time in England before returning to his home village to lead mountain expeditions. He told us that the villagers were curious how we could be so far into the mountains with only enough supplies for a day hike. They also invited us to spend the night if we needed shelter. I respond that our base camp was just over the ridge and we planned to be back before dark.

Then an older villager stepped up and spoke in broken English. "Welcome. I am the village doctor. The last time I recall someone wandering into our village with only enough supplies for the day—it must have been close to forty years ago. He was a young man and was also English."

"On second thought, I think we will accept the invitation to stay for the evening," I replied "We would love to learn more about your village and that visitor."

This evening, one of the families served us a meal that was both filling and warming. I am not certain what we were eating, but the flavors were quite exotic and all of us enjoyed the meal and conversation. When we finished, the guide said that they were all interested in our expedition and what brought us to their village. I was more anxious to hear about the last visitor who had visited with only day provisions, but I started out by telling them about our search for the Yeti. Then I told them that my father had made a similar search many years back and we believed he may have made his way into their valley. The village doctor had joined us for the meal and I asked what he remembered of the other Englishman that passed through.

He said that many years ago, a young man had wandered into their village with only day hiking gear. He was dazed from the bump on his head and had blood on his face and shirt. It appeared that he had taken a bad fall during his trek. The villagers brought him to the physician who cared for the stranger until he was well enough to travel again. The doctor determined that the bump had erased the man's memory. Not only could he not recall where his base camp was located, but the man had no recollection of who he was or even what he was doing in the mountains. When he was well enough to travel, the doctor accompanied him back to Kathmandu and suggested he find his way back to England. The doctor did not know what became of him after that.

I believe the wandering man was Reginald. Now we know he survived his search for the Yeti but not what happened to him after he reached Kathmandu. If he did not regain his memory, we can only hope that he made his way back to the Isles. Perhaps he is even there now and has a new life. Tomorrow we will return to the cave, collect our supplies and return to Kathmandu.

Tuesday, June 28

This morning we left the village and hiked back over the ridge to the cave. Nana excitedly greeted us and signed that she and her uncle worried when we did not return yesterday but passed the time catching up on old family stories. I told Nana what we learned about Reginald and that we decided to end the expedition and return to England. I asked her to invite her uncle to return with us and that he would be welcome to live on the Shockpocket estate.

Nana relayed the message to her uncle and they chattered back and forth for several minutes. Finally, she signed that he was very thankful for the invitation but preferred to stay in his mountain home. He had made such an effort to escape from mankind and spent so many years on his own that he did not think he'd be happy anywhere than in the mountains by himself. He only asked that we might make the occasional trip to Nepal to visit him in his cave home. We promised that we would.

Today is Katherine's birthday and this evening we celebrated with a wide selection of local dishes and sweets that we had brought back from the village. Nana once again played her bagpipes and we all danced around the campfire. What a brilliant celebration! In the morning we start back for Kathmandu.

Thursday, June 30

We have returned to Kathmandu for a well-deserved rest before we start back for England. As we checked into the inn, I told the innkeeper what had happened in the mountains and looked in the registration book again to see if we could find another signature with Reginald's handwriting. Upon reexamination of the pages, we found a signature that looked similar to Reginald's. It read: *Mr. English.*

I am now hopeful that Reginald set out for England in hopes of finding his identity. On one hand, I consider the expedition a success. We know more about the disappearance of Reginald Shockpocket than before. We also may have solved the mystery of the Himalayan snow creature.

Unfortunately, once again we have made a scientific expedition and have nothing to show for it. Well, that is not exactly true. We brought back some some splendid Yak wool sweaters and caps plus a box of wonderful Masala Chai tea. And I think Shockpockets Miracle Ski Wax will be a very successful product. In order to avoid poor publicity, we have decided not speak of this expedition to anyone upon our return to England.

Saturday, July 2

This morning, on our walk down to the inn's dining room for breakfast, I found on the desk today's Nepal edition of the *London Times*, and on the front page a large headline proclaiming:

London Times Exclusive
Second Shockpocket Expedition Fails

Tweak shouted, "How could the London Times know about the expedition and its outcome? It was a secret."

The article read:

Today, an undisclosed source informed the London Times that Thaddeaus Shockpocket recently undertook another secret expedition, this time to the Himalayas in search of the Yeti, a hairy creature that some say lives in the remote mountain areas of Nepal. It appears that the expedition was another failure for the Shockpockets. Reports from Kathmandu say that he brought back no evidence of the beast.

This newspaper has not yet reached Professor Shockpocket for comment.

Sherlock finished reading and said, "The innkeeper must have wired the news to London as soon as we returned. He is the only one that knows why we are here and that we did not find the Yeti."

I said, "Come to think of it, when we checked back into the inn a few days ago, there was another man in the lobby that may have overheard our conversation with the innkeeper. He was sitting by the window, his face hidden behind the newspaper he was reading. Now I am certain that we are being followed. But why? And by whom?"

Tweak answered, "I bet it is Wallace Bogglesworth. He just wants to embarrass you."

Then Katherine spoke up, "Oh, I certainly hope not. Contrary to appearances, Wallace and your father are still friends. He may not support Thaddeaus' methods, but that is no reason for him to have us followed and then report on our failures."

I wanted to agree with Kate, "Could Wallace really want to win the Victoria Medal so badly that he would go out of his way to discredit us? I also hope that is not true. But if it is, he has just put an end to a long and special friendship."

Tomorrow we begin our drive home, not sure what to expect when we arrive. The world knows that we have once again failed in an attempt to win the Victoria Medal. I do not know whether to confront Wallace or simply move on.

Mr. English

Monday, August 1

Our travel back to England was without incident, although it seemed to take forever with the cloud of failure once again hanging over our heads. When we arrived home, there were several letters waiting for us. Some of them offered condolences on yet another doomed expedition, some said to give up, and a few offered encouragement. But one letter was to change our lives forever. It read:

Dear Thaddeaus Shockpocket,

You do not know me as such, but I ask that you please read my letter in its entirety. It contains information that I hope you will be happy to receive. I believe it is a miracle.

Several weeks ago, I was reading the London Times and spotted a short piece about your recent attempt to find the Yeti. I am a fellow practitioner of science and felt that any article spotlighting a fellow researcher's failure was extremely bad sport and uncalled for. Unlike you, my current field of study is botany. I have worked for many years in the greenhouse and various fields breeding plants for new medicinal remedies and I like to say that I am helping to develop products to better the world.

At any rate, as angry as the London Times story made me, I quickly put it out of my mind and returned to my gardening. I have been having problems with rabbits eating my special plants and am trying to develop a method to eradicate the little pests. A few days after reading the article, I began having the strangest dreams. Nothing like my typical dreams of flowers and bees and rabbits and such. In these dreams I seemed to be imagining what it must be like to be a world explorer like you, right down to being on a trek in the mountains.

I know you are probably thinking 'what do this man's dreams have to do with me?' but this is where it becomes interesting. As the nightly dreams continued, they became more vivid. In the beginning, I was simply sitting in a cave and cooking over a camp stove. Nothing more. Then, the dreams became longer and seemed to take a humorous turn. I dreamt that I had a pet bear in the cave with me and that I would feed him as he lay next to me on the floor. One night the dream became very long and very detailed. This time, I felt that I was in the mountain cave for a specific reason, but I could not quite figure it out. There was no longer a bear in the cave with me, but instead a bear blanket lying on the cave floor. For some unknown reason, I wanted to leave the cave and hike up the long white hill above it. I did so and at the top of the hill I could see a village in the next valley and started to walk down the snowfield towards it. As I reached the midpoint of my descent I tripped and started rolling out-of-control towards a cluster of rocks near the bottom. I was unable to stop and the dream ended as the world was spinning and I woke up screaming.

Dear Thaddeaus, this is where the miracle occurs. When I awoke, I realized that I had just regained memories of my entire life. You see, up to that night I only knew that I had suffered an accident many years ago and it had left me with no memories. Immediately after the accident, I was only aware that I was wandering through Europe and needed to return to my homeland, which I believed to be England, as that was the language I spoke. Once I reached England, I did not know what village or town I came from so I moved from village to village until I was taken in by a nice family in Ravenstonedale and I have lived here since. At first I simply tended the family's gardens but then I found that I have a talent for breeding hybrid plants and that became my passion.

By now you may have guessed what I remember and what I consider to be a miracle. I now know that I am Reginald Shockpocket, your father. I can clearly remember playing with you as a young lad and all of our fishing trips to Loch Ness. Now that my memories are back, I realize how much I miss you and your mother, Fiona, and I would like to reunite as soon as possible. I hope you are as happy to discover this as I am. With your permission, I would like to visit the Shockpocket estate in the near future and become reacquainted with my family. You need not worry that I am coming to reclaim the estate. I know that our family has undoubtedly moved on and changed since my accident. I only wish to reunite with my loved ones.

All my love,
Reginald Shockpocket AKA Mr. English

My hands quivered as I set the letter down.

"Katherine, I need a cup of Chamomile tea."

Kate looked concerned, "Thaddeaus, what is it?"

I held the letter up, "I suggest you brew us both a strong cup and then read this for yourself."

Katherine left to put the pot on in the kitchen and I read the letter again. After all these years of wondering what had become of my father, the news of his whereabouts was overwhelming. And what's more, the village of Ravenstonedale is not a long distance from the Shockpocket estate. If not for his reading about my search for the Yeti, we may never have discovered each other and continued to live only a few miles apart.

Katherine returned to the study with two steaming cups of tea and set them on the end table before picking up the letter laying there. My hands still shook as I lifted my cup and tried to take a sip of hot tea. This resulted in most of the tea ending up on my shirt instead of in my mouth.

By the time Katherine completed the letter, not only were her hands trembling but her eyes were overflowing with tears. "Oh, Thaddeaus this is a miracle! You must answer your father straight away and invite him to visit as soon as possible."

I agreed. "As soon as my hands settle a bit. I need another cup of Chamomile first. It will do more good in my stomach than on my clothes."

Tuesday, August 9

I sent a letter to Reginald last week and he is visiting the Shockpocket estate tomorrow. I also sent a telegraph message to my mother in Colorado and she replied that she was booking passage to England with greatest haste. Given good connections, she should be here within the next two weeks. Sherlock and Tweak are beside themselves with excitement. This is a most wondrous time for the Shockpocket family.

Friday, August 19

Reginald and Fiona both made their way to the Shockpocket estate safely and the Shockpocket family reunion has been absolutely brilliant. At our first dinner as a full family, Reginald recounted his life over the last thirty years and how he had developed several hybrid flowers used to treat a wide range of common ailments. I told him about my own botanical studies and how I invented the SHARE animal relocation device to keep the gardens rabbit free. During the meal and after, mother mostly stared at Reginald with misty eyes and kept repeating that she always knew the love of her life would come back.

While we ate dessert, I asked him what he remembered about his search for the Yeti and he filled us in on details that had not been recorded in his journal. When he finished, we told him all about our own expedition and how we had retraced his original route. I said that it was a miracle that the *London Times* newspaper article had triggered his memories, but shared that the article was also cause for some concern as it would suggest that we were being followed and our activities reported to the newspaper. I confided that we had spotted a mysterious man at both Loch Ness and in Kathmandu and, further, that I thought Wallace Boggelsworth was having us followed in order to discredit my reputation.

When I made the comment about Wallace my mother spoke up and said that it could not be him. She noted that she was an exceptional judge of character and, based on her memory of Wallace, would stake her name on his not being the one having us followed. She said that no matter how angry he may have been at my ruining his Egyptian dig expedition, he was not the type of person that would try to discredit me to get even. I said I was not so sure and that I planned to hire an investigator to find the culprit who was following us. I would also find out who hired him and have both of them tossed into jail.

At that point, my mother began choking uncontrollably. Sherlock ran over and patted her back until she regained her breath and sputtered, "Thaddeaus, are you sure that is the best course of action? Perhaps whoever was having you followed was only looking out for your safety and trying to protect you."

"Then why did they send those articles to the newspaper?" I asked.

She answered, "Perhaps he didn't know that the person he hired would also send reports to the newspaper. Perhaps that was not part of their agreement and the person following you sent the updates to the London Times on his own to earn extra money."

I stared at her. "Then why didn't the person having me followed tell them to stop after the Loch Ness article?"

Her face was turning red, "Well, perhaps they do not live in Europe. And they do not read the London Times. So they did not see the articles..." Her voice drifted off.

I was getting frustrated with my mother and thought that her imagination was getting the best of her. "That is crazy. What person from another country would have me followed to protect me, hire someone he did not know well and who he obviously couldn't trust, and then not know that his employee was sending news of my failures to the London Times to make a little extra money."

The room was silent for a few moments, and then all eyes turned to Fiona.

Her face had turned an even darker shade of red, "Now, Thaddy, don't get angry. You may be a grown man and world explorer, but you are still my son and"

Sherlock interrupted: "*Thaddy*?"

Tweak giggle uncontrollably. "Our daddy is *Thaddy*?"

Kate said "Hush" and then snickered to herself. "I haven't heard her call you that in years."

Fiona spoke louder and said firmly, "All of you, hush! I love my Thaddy—okay, *Thaddeaus*—and I worry about him. We all know that your father occasionally misses minor details in his work and we all also know that these slips have led to unexpected consequences, some rather dire. I was only trying to watch out for all of you. When you wrote to me of your planned crypto-zoological expeditions, I contacted a friend in London and asked him to find someone to follow you for your own safety. My friend found this advertisement in the newspaper."

She pulled out a torn square of newsprint.

THADDEAUS SHOCKPOCKET: VICTORIA

Discreet Investigative Services

Are you suspicious of someone's activities? Would you like them followed? Then hire me, Guy Shifty, master of deception, disguise and tracking. Whatever they are up to, I will find out and you will know. Trust me.

"Mr. Shifty was only to follow you and get involved if you were in danger and needed assistance. I did not ask for reports and had no idea he would send news of your failures to the newspaper. I am so very sorry. Please forgive me."

I thought about Fiona's words and all eyes now turned to me. I sat thinking for a moment before I was abruptly kicked under the table by not only Katherine, but also Tweak and Sherlock.

"Yes, yes, I forgive you mother," I said. "It is just that I was so angry at Wallace. I thought he was the one having me followed. I never imagined it was you."

Sunday, August 21

I have decided to abandon my quest for the Victoria medal in cryptozoology and refocus on the conventional sciences. After all, we know the Unicorn did exist, but cannot prove it. We know that the Loch Ness serpent does exist, but do not want to prove it. And we think the Yeti may not exist, but will let Nana's uncle continue to have fun scaring the locals in the mountains of Nepal. That is enough for now. Yesterday I sent a letter to Wallace telling him of my decision and wishing him luck on his upcoming expedition.

Wednesday, August 31

I have received a reply letter from Wallace regarding my decision not to make any more cryptozoological expeditions. He wrote that he was glad to hear that I will discontinue my pursuit of myths and will focus on legitimate areas of study. He adds that he never really had a problem with me as a friend and scientist, just with some of my pursuits and methods. Finally, and I had to read this part of his letter twice to believe it, he says that he wants to give me another chance to assist him. He will soon be opening an Egyptian crypt that he believes is of upmost importance. If I promise not to do anything stupid, he would like me to join him and, once again, attempt to analyze the contents of the canopic jars to see what questions they may answer about the Egyptians.

This is wonderful news. The expedition leaves in one week. If all goes well I will return home in early October. I do not need to make major preparations other than to pack my chemical analysis kit.

The Winner Is...

Saturday, December 10

Today the ceremony to announce the winner of the Victoria Medal took place on the front steps of the Royal Society of Scientific Research and Global Exploration, exactly where the competition began one year ago. It seems like only yesterday that we gathered on these same steps to hear the list of contenders for the Victoria Medal. Once again, the wooden podium with E.R.S.S.R.G.E. banner was positioned at the top of the stairway and, once again, the members of the judging committee stood to each side. But the atmosphere today was even more celebratory. The crowd of onlookers waved British flags and the band played loudly as the excitement built to hear who would be the winner of the Victoria Medal. Dr. Beakersniff stepped up to the podium and raised his hand. The crowd became so quiet, only the shuffling of feet on the cobblestone street could be heard.

Dr. Beakersniff announced, "It is indeed my great pleasure and honor to announce the first winner of the Royal Society of Scientific Research and Global Exploration Victoria Medal for greatest scientific achievement or discovery of the year. The award goes to Wallace Bogglesworth for his discovery of an important Egyptian tomb with all of its treasures still intact. His discovery will enable us to learn more of the society of the ancient Egyptians."

The crowd erupted in cheers as Wallace stepped to the podium to receive the medal.

Then, Dr. Beakersniff raised his hand again, "I would also like to announce that the committee has decided to award a second Victoria Medal this year." He paused for effect. "For his valuable contribution to the research conducted at the Bogglesworth Egyptian dig, I am honored to award Thaddeaus Shockpocket a Victoria Medal for his chemical analysis of canopic jars containing preserved mummy organs. His diligent work and focus on details revealed the secrets of the mummy's health, his diet, and how he died. Contrary to common belief that the pharaoh was killed by those wanting to take his power, we now know he most likely died from eating an undercooked pigeon."

The crowd roared and waved their flags as I joined Wallace at the podium to receive my medal. Flash powder from a dozen newspaper cameras went off as Wallace and I shook hands and held our medals up for the entire crowd to see, and the band struck up a celebratory tune.

After the award ceremony, we all celebrated at a local café. As we left the café some time later we spotted a newsstand with the latest edition of the *London Times* hot off of the press.

Bogglesworth and Shockpocket Win

Today, the scientific team of Wallace Bogglesworth and Thaddeaus Shockpocket were awarded Victoria Medals for scientific discovery and achievement of the year. The work of this duo was particularly special as it not only uncovered a wealth of Egyptian artifacts that will keep Egyptologists busy for years, but also the detailed chemical analysis of the mummy's remains found in canopic jars can reveal detailed new information about those buried.

When reached for comment Thaddeaus Shockpocket said that he had always admired Dr. Bogglesworth's work and was honored to have been a part of this historic expedition. Wallace Bogglesworth noted that he expects Thaddeaus to be a key member of his team on future digs.

Uncle Nick

Friday, December 30

The mail has been pouring in since the announcement of the award. Most are letters of congratulation, several are senders proposing new experiments for me to try, and some ask for employment. Today, as I shuffled through the fresh stack of letters, I spotted one from a dear old friend in the United States and I knew that I needed to open it first. But before I tell of the letter, I must provide a bit more of my family history and how I came to know this special friend.

This story begins when my father, Reginald, was just a young man beginning his scientific career. He made an expedition to the United States of America in search of dinosaur bones. At that time, new discoveries were being made on a regular basis, many of them in the state of Colorado, and that is where he set off in hopes of making a discovery of great value. Shortly after arriving he met Fiona, who was assisting her father with his own dig. Her parents were also bone hunters and had moved to the United States from Ireland shortly before she was born. The first time Reginald saw Fiona with her flaming red hair, he fell instantly in love. Luckily for Reginald, the feelings were mutual. The young woman was completely taken with the new English archeologist at the dig site. Within a few months the two became engaged and Reginald returned to England with his new American bride. Reginald did not find any unique dinosaur bones but left Colorado feeling that his discovery of Fiona more than made up for it.

Years later, when Reginald disappeared during his search for the Yeti, Fiona returned to Colorado Springs where her family could help her raise me. She shuttered up the Shockpocket estate and told me that it would be there for me when I reached adulthood should I decide to move back to England. I lived with my mother in Colorado Springs from the time I was eight until I returned to England at twenty years of age. Back in England, I continued my education, met Katherine, and have lived here ever since. In the years since I returned to England, I have regularly visited my mother in Colorado. Katherine, Sherlock, and Tweak accompany me on these visits and our entire family is close to Grandmother Fiona and her friends there.

Why am I telling you all of this? Well, one of those friends sent the letter that now sits in front of me. We call him Uncle Nick and I have admired him from the time of our first meeting. My mother and I met Nick one evening when we took dinner at our favorite restaurant in Colorado Springs. I remember that evening as clear as if it were yesterday.

I was sixteen at the time and our weekly dinners at the restaurant were a treat my mother never missed. One evening as we ate, a tall thin man entered and sat by himself at a table to the side of the room. Fiona took pity on the stranger and invited him to join us. He was hesitant at first, but then joined us at our table and that led to one of the most amazing evenings of my life. The gentleman told us that he was a scientist and had just moved to Colorado Springs to conduct experiments. My mother told him about my father and how he had disappeared on a scientific expedition. Nick explained that his science was of quite a different nature and all took place within his laboratories. He explained that he experimented with electricity and had already made several great discoveries in the area of electrical transmission. He was now attempting to transmit electricity through the air in a laboratory just outside of town.

I asked if I could see his laboratory. He resisted at first but finally gave in to my begging. I was to become a regular visitor to his laboratory outside of town. I loved watching his experiments and how he would create lighting inside of his laboratory. After that first evening, Nick joined us for our weekly dinners at the hotel and I learned about the science of electricity. After a few months, he told us that his work at the local laboratory was finished and he was returning to the East Coast. In spite of his leaving, we have stayed in touch and I consider him a good friend to this day. In fact, Tweak is named after him as her full name is Tesla Winifred Katherine Shockpocket.

So, there in front of me sat a letter with the return address for Nicola Tesla. I always enjoy Nick's letters and hearing of his latest discoveries and I opened the letter anxiously.

Dear Thaddeaus,

I hope this letter finds you well. I want to congratulate you on winning the Victoria Medal. Your mother told me of the award and the even greater news that you have found your long lost father. I hope you have a wonderful reunion.

When do you, Katherine and the children plan to visit the United States again? I recently read in a scientific journal that you had developed a chemo electric plasma elephant stun gun. I find this most intriguing and would like to learn more about your device. As you know, I have spent many years attempting to transmit electricity wirelessly. Perhaps you have discovered a method that will make this possible. Please let me know when you will be traveling this way again as I would like to share ideas with you and see if we can solve some of the hurdles I keep encountering. Perhaps your entire family could join you and we can all share stories of our scientific endeavors. Give my best to the family.

Nikola Tesla

DEAR READER

WHAT A BRILLIANT TURN OF EVENTS WE HAVE ENJOYED. WALLACE AND I ARE AGAIN WORKING TOGETHER AND BOTH OF US HAVE VICTORIA MEDALS FOR OUR EFFORTS, AND FIONA AND REGINALD ARE REUNITED AND HAVE DECIDED TO RETURN TO FIONA'S HOME IN COLORADO SPRINGS. KATHERINE AND I HAVE AGREED TO ACCOMPANY THEM ON THEIR JOURNEY HOME AND WE WILL ALL TRAVEL ABOARD OUR AIRSHIP, ALBION 77. WHILE WE ARE IN THE UNITED STATES, WE WILL MAKE TIME TO VISIT UNCLE NICK. I MUST SAY THAT I AM ANXIOUS TO SHARE MY PROGRESS IN THE AREA OF CHEMO ELECTRIC PLASMA WITH NIKOLA AND TO LEARN OF HIS ACHIEVEMENTS IN TRANSMITTING ELECTRICITY THROUGH THE AIR. I AM ESPECIALLY EXCITED TO SHARE MY PROGRESS ON THE PULSED MODULATION DUAL FREQUENCY TRANSLINEAR TIME WAVE SYNCHRONIZATION DEVICE. PERHAPS HE CAN HELP ME WITH THE LAST FEW HURDLES AND WE CAN TEST IT WHILE THERE. WHO KNOWS WHERE OR WHEN THAT WILL LEAD?

YOURS IN THE SPIRIT OF SCIENCE AND ADVENTURE,
THADDEAUS SHOCKPOCKET

Random Bits and Pieces

Canopic jars

Canopic jars are stone or clay jars used to store the body organs of people or animals being mummified.

Cryptozoology

Cryptozoology is the search for creatures of myths or legends, such as dragons, unicorns, and the Loch Ness monster.

Déjà vu

Déjà vu is the feeling that you have experienced something before.

Egyptology

Egyptology is the study of Egyptian history. Around the turn of the century, regular discoveries were being made in the field of Egyptology as new tombs were unearthed and researched.

Himalayas

The Himalayas are a mountain range in South Asia. They are home to the highest mountains in the world including Mount Everest with an altitude of 23,600 feet.

Jules Verne

Jules Verne was a French author and playwright. He is best known for his science fiction novels such as Journey to the Center of the Earth, Twenty Thousand Leagues Under the Sea, and Around the World in Eighty Days. Jules Verne lived from 1828 to 1905.

Kathmandu

Kathmandu is the largest city in Nepal and sits in a valley at an elevation of over four thousand feet. Nepal is a country located in South Asia in the Himalayas. Mount Everest is located in Nepal.

Masala Chai tea

Masala chai is a spice tea made by combining black tea with hot milk and a mixture of spices and herbs. These may include cinnamon, cardamom, peppercorns, fennel, clove, anise, and others depending on personal taste.

Mummification

Mummification is the process of preserving a body so that it does not decay after burial. Many people associate mummification with Egyptians, but the process has been used by many civilizations for thousands of years.

Nautilus

Nautilus is the name of the submarine featured in Jules Verne's two novels Twenty Thousand Leagues Under the Sea and The Mysterious Island. The fictional submarine was battery powered and featured many futuristic devices that did not exist at the time the books were written.

Nikola Tesla

Nikola Tesla was an engineer and inventor that made several discoveries relating to the transmission and use of electricity. Tesla lived from 1856 to 1943. At his laboratory outside of Colorado Springs, he conducted experiments involving transmitting electricity without wires.

Peanut Butter and Sardine Sandwich

Yumm. There is nothing quite like a peanut butter and sardine sandwich when out lolling about the countryside on a lazy afternoon. Here is my very own recipe.

Ingredients:

1. One (1) I – Jar Peanut Butter

2. Two (2) II - slices of bread. You may trim the crust if you prefer. Note: I would advise doing this if you don't plan to eat your crusts and are enjoying your meal near Loch Ness. Nessie is rather fond of peanut butter and sardine sandwich crusts and may interrupt your lunch if you through them in the water.

3. Three (3) III - nice canned sardines

Procedure:

First, lay both pieces of bread side by side. (This is when you may trim the crusts)

Second, spread peanut butter on BOTH pieces of bread. Spreading it on both pieces is important because the sardines will be surrounded by peanut butter and won't slip out of your sandwich.

Third, lay the sardines on one of the pieces of bread and place the other piece on top, peanut butter facing down.

Fourth, cut the sandwich in half or fourths.

Fifth, enjoy!!!

Queen Victoria

Victoria became Queen of the United Kingdom at the age of eighteen. Her reign lasted over 63 years, from 1837 to 1901, and is the longest of any king or queen in British history. This period is known as the Victorian era and is recognized as a period of exceptional exploration, scientific discovery, and advances in industry and technology.

Yak

Yaks can be found in the Himalayas and are a distant relative of cows. They have long hair and are valued for their fur, milk, and meat. They are also used as pack animals to carry supplies.

Yeti

The Yeti is also known as the abominable snowman and is said to be an ape like creature that lives in the Himalayan Mountains. No Yeti has ever been captured, but many people believe they have found footprints of the creature in the snow.

The Journals of Thaddeaus Shockpocket: Book 1—ALBION 77

Turn of the century English inventor and explorer Thaddeaus Shockpocket is having another bad day. It seems like only yesterday his ten-year-old son Sherlock was carried off into the jungle by local natives after Thaddeaus accidentally presented the boy as a gift to the local chief. And now it is happening again. He stands helplessly watching as his wife Katherine disappears into the sky in the family airship ALBION 77 after he accidentally pumped too much helium into the balloon.

Another shockpocket has been lost in the pursuit of science and one thought bursts into Thaddeaus' head, pushing out all others as he watches the pinpoint balloon vanish into the distance. "It's four o'clock. I hope Tweak put the kettle on. I need a nice cup of tea."

And then a second thought. "We really must go and find Sherlock."

And then a third. "I hope Katherine lands. Soon. And somewhere nice. What an adventure she will have. If only she doesn't crash first."

Yes, it is just another day in the Shockpocket family. But this day leads to unexpected discovery and adventure as Thaddeaus and his twelve-year-old daughter Tweak wait for word from Katherine, invent several new devices to change the world, and search for Sherlock in the deepest, darkest corners of Brazil.

Author Henry Walton has invented several products of questionable value over the years. None of these have made it to market. And that is probably for the better. His journeys through the Americas, Europe, Africa and Asia have led him to the epic conclusion – The world is Absolutely Brilliant. Difficult sometimes. Confusing often. But humorous almost always. Thaddeaus Shockpocket is Henry's book series for young adults.

Illustrator William Kevin Petty studied archeology and worked in museums during his 20's. His love of history, science and technology combined with world travel while in the service shaped his techno-whimsical illustration style and made him the perfect selection for Thaddeaus Shockpocket. Kevin has illustrated several books and posters in the Steampunk genre.

40322805R00092

Made in the USA
Charleston, SC
04 April 2015